HER
SUPER-SECRET
REBOUND
BOYFRIEND

HER SUPER-SECRET REBOUND BOYFRIEND

KERRI CARPENTER

Entangled Publishing, LLC
2614 South Timberline Road
Suite 105, PMB 159
Fort Collins, CO 80525
rights@entangledpublishing.com

Lovestruck is an imprint of Entangled Publishing, LLC.

Edited by Alethea Spiridon
Cover design by Fiona Jayde
Cover art from iStock

Manufactured in the United States of America

First Edition June 2018

To all those Saturday nights spent with Nunnie watching The Golden Girls.

Chapter One

"Crying is for plain women. Pretty women go shopping."
-Blanche Devereaux

"Everything you need to know about life you can learn by watching *The Golden Girls*."

Lola raised an eyebrow at her best friend and roommate. Frankie meant well, but sometimes it took a little time and patience to figure out exactly what she was talking about.

"I'm serious," Frankie said after she snagged the carton of double-chocolate fudge ice cream they were currently sharing.

One carton, two spoons, a Ryan Gosling movie marathon with your best friend. Not a bad way to spend a Saturday getting over a breakup. Of course, a better way to spend a Saturday would be hanging out with your boyfriend. Well, if he didn't just dump you for someone younger, prettier, and more fun.

"I know you're serious, Frankie, and I am well aware of your love affair with reruns of *The Golden Girls*. But I thought we were talking about me and all my lameness."

"You're not lame, Lola. I wouldn't be friends with you if you were. You got dumped."

"Thanks for reminding me." She shoveled a large spoonful of ice cream in her mouth.

"Let me finish. You got dumped and *The Golden Girls* are going to help you feel better. Trust me. Dorothy, Rose, Blanche, and Sophia know all."

Lola rolled her eyes. She couldn't help it. "Oh really. And just what would they say to make me feel better about Mark?"

"Mark is a douche. And anyway, it's not what they would say to you. It's what they would do. They have all the answers to the problems of the world."

Curious, Lola put her spoon and the now empty ice cream carton on the coffee table and turned to give her friend her full attention. After she paused *Crazy, Stupid, Love* first, of course.

Always dramatic, Frankie sat up straight, flipped her curly auburn hair over her shoulder, and took a deep breath. "Okay, so, think about it. *The Golden Girls* know how to live life. Number one. Get a great roommate."

Frankie shimmied her shoulders and made a kissy face. Lola laughed.

"Obviously, you already have that one down," Frankie said. "Next," she said, holding up two fingers, "cheesecake makes everything better. Third…"

"If you tell me to start dating every guy I meet like Blanche or your next sentence starts with 'Picture it…Sicily', I'm going to throw up."

It was Frankie's turn to laugh. "No. Although, Blanche may have been on to something. She loved her body, she was confident, and she enjoyed dating. Hmm, all things you don't possess."

"Shut up." Lola threw a pillow at her.

She did enjoy dating. Lola preferred being in a committed relationship to randomly hooking up. As a homebody, her preference was to spend the night with her boyfriend cooking together and binging Netflix rather than getting hammered at a bar and making idle chitchat with some douchey guy who smelled like beer and wore too much aftershave.

Frankie, on the other hand, loved going out. She was always the first to try a new bar or get them VIP passes to the hottest club. Frankie was an expert flirter, and men always seemed to flock to her. If she wanted, she could be out with any of the twenty guys who'd snapped her in the last week. All she had to do was bat her pretty eyelashes. Even when she broke up with someone, he was still enamored with her. She was almost to the friend limit on Facebook. Basically, she was Lola's polar opposite.

Although…there was something covetable about Frankie's love life. Lola saw it as almost freeing. Frankie was always smiling and laughing. Everyone loved her, and she was the life of the party. Not that Lola didn't have friends and a life. She did. It was just a small, quiet life.

She glanced at Frankie and saw the determination on her face. Lola wasn't getting out of this conversation.

"I'm sure there's some point to all of this," Lola said. "Why don't you just get to it?"

"My point is that you are bummed because Mark dumped you."

"I know this already, Francesca."

Frankie stuck her tongue out at the use of her full name. "Mark was a loser, and you need to get back out there and have some fun. Life is too short. You're young, you're smart, you're totally gorgeous."

Lola caught a glimpse of her reflection in the window behind the couch. Her long brown hair probably needed a trim, although she liked how her bangs had grown out to that perfect length and touched the tip of the black glasses she absolutely needed to wear. Frankie always said her light-blue eyes were so pretty and how she should lose the glasses. But Lola had tried contacts, and glasses were more comfortable. Besides, as a librarian, she was constantly staring at books and computer screens. Contacts tended to dry up and become itchy by the end of the workday.

"I know what you're thinking, Lola Susan McBride. You're going to tell me that you're not gorgeous, even though you have the body of a Victoria's Secret model. Damn you," she added for good measure.

"Oh please," Lola said with one last look at her reflection. She was plain and boring. If she really resembled a model, Mark wouldn't have broken up with her. Well, probably not.

"And it's time for you to take that bangin' body out there, dress it up in provocative clothes, have some fun, and find a super-hot rebound guy."

"You know I'm not going to do any of that. Besides, I wouldn't even know how. Or where to go."

Frankie's eyes were practically sparkling. "Well...you could do speed dating."

Lola scrunched up her nose.

Frankie laughed. "Okay, that's out. We could barhop next weekend. Ooh, you could go back on Tinder or Bumble."

Lola groaned. Like most single people, she'd tried online dating. She'd been on a fair amount of dates and even had a relationship with someone from OKCupid for a couple months. But she'd also been stood up twice, suffered through a date with a man she was pretty sure was batting for the other team, and received three dick pics.

The idea of returning to that Pandora's box of fun? No thank you.

"Lola, you have to put yourself out there. It's a numbers game. The more men you meet, the better your chances of finding someone."

"But I don't know how to do that," Lola whined.

"I do," Frankie said in a singsong voice. "And so do Dorothy, Rose, Blanche, and Sophia."

"Are we back to that?"

"We never left. Didn't you see the episode where they crashed someone else's high school reunion?"

Because of Frankie's love of *The Golden Girls*, Lola had seen pretty much every episode at least three times. "Doesn't Dorothy become...wait a minute. You're not suggesting we crash a high school reunion?"

Frankie's grin spread from ear to ear.

Lola jumped up and shook her head. "No, no, no."

Frankie joined her off the couch. "Yes, yes, yes. And I know just the high school."

"It better not be one of the high schools here in Arlington."

"As a matter of fact, Kennedy is having their ten-year reunion tonight."

"Nope, uh-uh."

"Kennedy is the perfect school. There were like two thousand kids in each class. No way did everyone know each other. We'll wait until the reunion has started, grab a nametag off the table, and then blend right in."

"Don't those nametags belong to alums attending their reunion?" Not that Lola was actually considering this ludicrous plan.

Frankie shook her head. "I know someone on the reunion committee at Kennedy."

Of course she did.

"They said they print out badges for every classmate whether they've RSVP'd or not. Come on, Lola. There's nothing to lose."

"How about my respect? My dignity?"

"Who cares about those things? We are going to live it up

and find you a hottie." Frankie clapped her hands excitedly. "You're going to have so much fun. Especially after the makeover I'm about to give you."

"Um, I haven't said yes yet."

When Lola took in Frankie's determined expression, she knew it didn't matter. Whether she liked it or not, she was going to a reunion. And it wasn't her own.

Two hours later, they stood outside Kennedy High School. Lola had been plucked, teased, and made over in every way imaginable. She was wearing one of Frankie's blue dresses that was about six inches too short, although Frankie insisted she show off her legs. She had to admit that her makeup *did* look good. The colors Frankie used brought out the blue in her eyes, and she loved the pink lipstick from Frankie's collection.

"You look amazing, Lola. There's still time to lose the glasses though."

"No way." That was the one place where Lola had to put her foot down.

"Fine, the glasses just add to the whole sexy librarian vibe."

Lola groaned. "You know I hate that stereotype. It's clichéd."

"And true. I mean, my God. Look at you. I'd totally make out with you in the stacks."

"Shut up." But she laughed as she said it.

They turned to take in the large high school. People were milling about, and they could already hear music filtering out from the gym.

"Looks like our reunion is in full swing." Frankie wiggled her eyebrows. "Let's go Bears!"

Lola rolled her eyes. "They're the Bobcats."

"Oh, whatever. I can't wait to get inside and see all of our friends from high school."

Lola shook her head as Frankie linked their arms and dragged her toward the door. "You are ridiculous."

Lola sighed. She had a feeling she wasn't going to like this. Even if Dorothy, Rose, Blanche, and Sophia had been there with her. She wasn't going to like this one bit.

• • •

Luke had a feeling he wasn't going to like this.

Going to his ten-year high school reunion wasn't his idea of a good time, but he'd promised some friends he would make it. Since he'd recently returned to Arlington, Virginia, after stints in both San Francisco and New York, he had no excuse. His old high school was only four miles from his current condo.

It wasn't like he hadn't enjoyed high school. In fact, Luke had a great time playing baseball, being goofy with his friends, and, of course, dating. He'd been one person in a very large class with his pick of beautiful dates.

He pushed through the front doors and made his way toward the gym. Ten years later and he could still navigate these hallways with his eyes closed. The place smelled the same, like pencil erasers and heavy-duty cleaner. Although, everything seemed smaller somehow.

Right outside the gym, he saw a long table set up with about a million nametags. He smiled at the two women manning the table, found his nametag, and made his way into the gym.

Already a good number of people were on the dance floor, moving to a song from their senior year of high school. Luke imagined the whole night would be filled with old-school songs and memories of yesteryear. Fine by him. While this wasn't exactly his favorite way to spend a Saturday night, he was looking forward to catching up with some of his friends. Speaking of, he saw one of his buddies making his way toward him.

"Ryan, great to see you." The two grabbed hands and pulled each other in for a brisk man-hug.

"You too, man. Wasn't sure you'd make it. You seemed kind of down on the reunion."

Luke shrugged. "You know how it is. It will be great to see the old crew. But the rest of these people…" He gestured around the gym that was becoming more packed by the second.

"I hear ya. Who the hell are all these people?" Ryan laughed.

They caught up for a few more minutes and were joined by more guys from their crew, Tyler, Jamal, and Oliver, who brought beers for all of them. Luke had to admit that it was nice to catch up. He was already laughing more than he had since returning to Arlington.

"So, what made you move back?" Jamal asked.

"He missed me so much he just had to come home," Oliver said.

Oliver had been his best friend since kindergarten. And he had missed him over the years, not that he'd admit that out loud.

Luke tipped his beer back and took a long slug. "Got a great job."

"Luke Evans, architect. Who would have thought it?"

"Yeah," Tyler added. "What happened to that whole professional baseball career?"

"Dick." Luke punched him on the arm. "And what happened to your dream of being a ballerina?"

"Now who's the dick," Tyler said, and the other three

guys all laughed.

"Language, language."

Luke turned to see a petite blonde saunter over with a big smile and eyes that were clearly only made for Tyler. She wrapped her arm around him.

"Everyone, this is my fiancé, Lacey. Lacey, these are the guys."

"Ah yes, the guys. Of course." She smiled. "I've heard a lot about you."

"I saw it on Facebook and I read your group text, but I still can't believe you're taking the plunge," Luke said.

"You should try it. Water's nice and warm. It's not a bad life. Having someone to come home to every night."

Oliver snorted. "Yeah, right. It's only been ten years since high school and already you forgot how averse Luke is to dating."

"Hey, hey, hey. I am not averse to dating. I love dating. I love women. I just don't do commitment. Never have. Never will."

As the guys laughed, Luke took a moment to peruse the gym. He recognized a person here or there. He liked that the reunion committee had blown up different photos from their high school yearbook and hung them around the room.

His phone vibrated in his pocket. Pulling it out, he rolled his eyes at the text message from his sister Mia.

Why haven't you asked Gretchen out yet?

Luke stifled the sigh that wanted to surface. He had three sisters. All three of them had jobs and busy lives, and yet they really seemed to enjoy spending their time trying to set up him. Coupled with their mother, the whole family wanted to see Luke married off.

He quickly typed back, *I've been busy at work.*

Mia made quick work with her reply. *If you had a serious girlfriend you wouldn't work so much.*

Luke loved work. He loved to date, too. What he didn't love was being pressured to ask some woman out who would then expect him to fall into a serious relationship. Before he knew it, he would be spending his Saturdays shopping for window treatments. There would be Sunday brunches in Adams Morgan and game night with other couples. He'd have to plan a Virginia winery trip and a weekend at a bed and breakfast in Annapolis. Next would come meeting the family followed by sharing holidays. Next thing he knew, he was married, tied down, getting a dog—not that he would mind the dog—and then came two-point-five children and a minivan. Luke did not do minivans. No thank you.

At the same time, he hated men who played with women, so he made a point of being as upfront as possible. He always explained that he wasn't looking for anything serious. Luke thought this was an admirable trait. Apparently, when word made it back to his sisters, they just tried harder to fix him up with someone new.

He rolled his shoulders. He didn't want to think about his sisters or their feeble attempts to penetrate his casual, carefree existence. Luckily, he spotted a large table with food in the back of the room. He excused himself from his friends and made his way toward it. Just as he was about to pop one of those delicious little Swedish meatballs into his mouth, he froze.

At the table next to him, he spotted the back of a gorgeous brunette in a super-short blue dress. The reunion committee was already hard at work raising money for their fifteen-year reunion—something he couldn't even wrap his mind around—by holding a raffle. There were baskets and items throughout the gym. The hot brunette was checking out a basket with a bunch of old-looking books in it.

She was probably about five-four or five-five, with long, shapely legs that disappeared into the short hem of that killer dress. From the back, she had a perfect hourglass figure. His mouth watered more than it had when he'd spotted the meatballs. Plus, all that long hair.

Her friend sauntered up to her then and noticed him checking her out.

Uh-oh, busted.

Luke tried to appear interested in the food once again, as the hot brunette's friend elbowed her and then whispered something. He pretended to study the large bowl of spinach artichoke dip while he strained to overhear the women's conversation, which seemed to be a bit of an argument. The only words he caught were *hot guy*, *over there*, *give me*, and he thought *glasses*. Then he was absolutely positive he heard one of them say *The Golden Girls*.

But before he could process that, the hot brunette spun around. It seemed like she may have been pushed. He didn't care, though, when he took in her gorgeous face. Pouty lips painted a vibrant pink, high cheekbones, and flawless skin. Plus, he was a sucker for women who had those bangs. There was something intriguing and mysterious about it.

She eyed him shyly, a blush coloring her cheeks. "Um, hi," she said, taking a step toward him.

He grinned. "Hey there."

Now that she was closer, he couldn't miss the crystal blue hue of her eyes. Beautiful. Luke had been around his share of gorgeous women over the years, but there was something different about this one. Something…genuine, he decided. At the same time as she was approaching him, she seemed nervous, as if this wasn't something she did often.

He had a thought. Maybe he knew her. Maybe they'd gone out in high school? Surely not. He'd remember someone who looked like this.

"Can you believe we're already having our ten-year reunion?" he asked.

"What? Oh, right. Yeah. I mean, no." She laughed. "I mean, no, I can't believe it's been ten whole years." She quickly averted her eyes.

She was adorable.

He stuck out a hand. "I'm Luke Erickson."

She shook his hand. "I'm Lo…" She glanced down at her nametag as if she needed a reminder. "I'm Kelli Martingale. Nice to meet you."

"I see you're interested in that basket over there."

She smiled, and the gesture lit up her whole face brighter than the overhead fluorescents that used to illuminate the hallways. Her eyes sparkled, and Luke sucked in a breath. If he thought she was hot before, he didn't even know a word to describe what he was seeing before him now.

At the mention of the raffle basket, Kelli became animated, her arms gesturing wildly. "Oh yes, I would give anything to win that. I know, it's probably dorky, but I'm totally—"

Her words were cut off when she stepped forward, hit the side of the table, shaking all the contents on it. Luke jumped to save a particularly wobbly red Jell-O dessert. He picked up the plate holding the dessert and turned to Kelli.

"Phew, that was a close one."

The words had just left his mouth when Kelli took another step, ran into him, causing most of the Jell-O mold to mold right onto his favorite white shirt.

Kelli gasped. "Ohmigod. I'm so sorry."

While he wanted to offer a huge *fuckkkkk*, he could tell that she felt horrible. So he shrugged as she quickly tried to help him clean up. Together, they got as much of the Jell-O off his shirt as they could. Then she grabbed a mound of napkins and began running them over his chest.

He shivered. Actually fucking shivered. What the hell? This Jell-O must be extra cold. Kelli must have felt it, too, because she paused, hands plastered against his chest, as she met his gaze. Her mouth fell open and formed an O.

Suddenly, it wasn't his shirt he was worried about; his pants began to feel a tad too snug. He wrapped his hands around her wrists and tried to offer a smile. Although, with the new, um, pain he was experiencing in his lower half, it probably came out as more of a grimace.

"I think I have it from here."

A red blush tinted her cheeks. "Of course. But I really am so sorry." She swore under her breath. Somehow, he could tell that she wasn't a big curser because as soon as the word left her lips, she scrunched up her nose and seemed surprised with herself. "I'll totally pay for dry cleaning."

"No worries."

Then she dug in her purse and pulled out a pair of thick black glasses.

"I'm not usually a klutzy person," she explained as she put the glasses on. "My roommate thought I looked sexier without my glasses, so she forced me to take them off. But I'm blind as a bat without them."

He took her in, and if he thought his pants were feeling tight before, he was pretty sure that all oxygen was leaving his body now. All he could say about the glasses was…holy fuck.

Her roommate thought she was sexier without them? Hells to the no. Definitely wrong on that one. The bombshell dress plus the thick sex kitten hair plus the gorgeous face plus the most seductive glasses in the history of eyewear equaled a speechless, hard Luke.

See, if Kennedy High taught him one thing, it was how to do math. Another equation was already becoming clear.

Kelli plus Luke was going to equal one hell of a reunion.

Chapter Two

"I hate to admit it, but he melts my Haagen-Dazs."
-Rose Nylund

"Welcome to Kennedy's ten-year class reunion." The crowd applauded and whistled.

Luke and Kelli both turned toward the stage. As the emcee was welcoming everyone, Luke tried to get his overactive libido in check. Hard to do when such a beautiful woman was standing close to him. Again, he thought about how he should remember someone who looked like her. He racked his brain trying to think of all the girls from his class.

"I'm sorry, but I can't quite place you." Something was niggling at the back of his mind. "What kind of stuff did you do in high school? Cheerleading? Soccer? Field hockey? Yearbook?"

She stared at a spot over his shoulder rather than meet his eyes. He also noticed she wrung her hands together like she was nervous. "Um, you know, like the usual stuff people did in high school."

Before he could follow up on that, the emcee caught his attention again.

"We're so excited that so many of you could come out tonight. We hope to see just as many, if not more, of you at our fifteen-year reunion. That's why we're already raising funds for it. Please continue to purchase raffle tickets, and we'll be doing drawings for the donated baskets throughout the night. Starting with our first one, the Jane Austen basket."

Next to him, Kelli gasped.

As the emcee explained the contents of the basket, his phone went off. He looked down to see a text message from his mother.

Don't forget about our family reunion next weekend.

Like his mom or sisters would let him forget about it. Still, it was fun to play with them. *What family reunion?* He wrote back.

Luke Cameron Erickson don't make me come find you. You know very well about the family reunion.

He chuckled silently. *Chill, Ma. Just kidding. I'll be there. With a date?*

Ma!

What? Can't a mother be curious?

He rolled his eyes, but suddenly the gym was clapping again.

"I can't believe it. I won!" Kelli shrieked.

"Hey, congrats. That's awesome." Although, he still wasn't sure why she was so excited about some Jane Austen books. Couldn't she go on Amazon and download them?

While she walked to the stage to claim her prize, a thought popped into his head, and he snapped his fingers. He did know Kelli Martindale. She'd moved to Arlington at the end of their junior year and had gone on three dates with Luke before she decided to date the head of the swim team.

He'd been moderately upset because Kelli had moved

from Alabama and had the most adorable Southern accent that had turned him on to no end. She'd also stood about five-ten, five-eleven with platinum blond hair. Which meant that the woman he'd been talking to wasn't Kelli Martindale. So who exactly was she? And why was she pretending to be someone else?

Oliver sauntered over to him then. "Hey, dude, who's the hottie?"

"Interesting question," Luke said. Oliver cocked his head in question. "I'm not sure yet."

Oliver waved his cell phone before pocketing it. "Before I forget, your sister keeps texting me."

"Which one?"

"Gwen. Keeps going on about some family reunion. Wanted me to remind you about it. There. Consider yourself officially reminded."

Luke groaned and offered Oliver a pained expression.

"What's your problem?" Oliver tipped back his beer. "I'll be there."

Luke stifled a laugh. "You'll be at my family reunion?"

"Wouldn't miss it."

"Shouldn't you stick to your own family?" He punched Oliver in the arm. His friend simply grinned.

Oliver had been part of his family since they were five years old, and he knew it. He was as welcome, if not more welcome, in the Erickson household than Luke. In fact, Luke knew that while he'd been living in other states, Oliver had kept an eye on his mom and sisters. He couldn't be more grateful to him.

"Hey, if my *abuela* wanted to have a reunion, I'd be there with bells on. Of course, it would only be the two of us so probably a pretty boring party. Unlike your crazy *familia*."

Oliver's mom had found out she was pregnant in high school. When she told the father, he'd broken up with her.

Shortly after Oliver was born, his mom left for greener pastures, too, and his grandmother raised him.

"And they are crazy. Especially my sisters. They all keep bugging me about this stupid reunion."

"They all want you to bring a date. What's up with that? I thought I was your date." Oliver blew him a kiss.

Luke punched him again. "Apparently, I'm 'of a certain age,' according to my mom. I wish they'd let me do my own thing."

"Like that smokin' hot brunette over there?" Oliver gestured toward the stage. Kelli was picking up her raffle basket. "Gonna tell me about her yet?"

"Her name's Kelli Martindale. Do you remember her?"

Oliver narrowed his eyes and peered in Kelli's direction. "Yes," he said, drawing out the word. "Kind of. I don't remember her looking like that. Of course, I was cute in high school but nothing like the fine specimen I am now." He flexed for effect.

"You're dreaming. So you don't think that's Kelli?"

"I dunno. Didn't you hook up with Kelli?"

Bingo. Luke grinned at the idea surfacing in his mind, but he had to be sure he was right. He decided to test "Kelli" on her Kennedy High School knowledge when she returned. When she began walking toward him again, Luke rushed Oliver off.

Carrying her basket, Kelli wore a huge smile.

"Congratulations," he said.

"Thank you. I adore Jane Austen. I can't believe someone donated these. They're really old editions and worth so much money."

That explained why she wanted the books so much. "You seem to know a lot about them."

"I'm a librarian, and I studied literature in college."

She kept talking, but all Luke could think about was the

fact that the arousing woman in front of him with the bangin'
body and alluring glasses was also a librarian. He'd never put
much into stereotypes, but the sexy librarian image was too
good to pass up.

"And that's why I can't believe I won this basket."

Luke frowned. A basket that was raising money for their
next reunion—a reunion he wasn't sure this woman should be
at. He had to go back to his original plan.

"Bet you loved the Jane Austen class junior year?"

"You had a Jane Austen class?" She caught herself. "I
mean, yeah, it was the best."

"I knew some people in that class. They held it in the west
building, right?"

"Um, yep. That's right."

"Who taught that class?" Luke asked.

"Oh, it was, um, Mrs., that is, Mrs…"

"Stark," he supplied. "Catelyn Stark, right?"

"That's right."

Luke grabbed her elbow and steered her away from the
crowd.

"What's going on?" she asked, still holding onto her
prized Jane Austen basket.

"Who are you really?" Luke asked, his eyes narrowing.

Her eyes widened. "I'm Kelli. Kelli Martindale."

"Oh really. That's interesting, considering that I've made
out with Kelli Martindale before. And that teacher of the
Jane Austen class I just made up? She's a character from
Game of Thrones."

She looked like a deer in headlights. "Oh. There was no
Jane Austen class?"

"Hell if I know. I was more into math."

"Oh."

"If you're not Kelli Martindale, who exactly are you?
And why lie?"

Then the whole story came tumbling out.

"The thing is, my boyfriend broke up with me last week, and I've been kinda bummed about it. So my roommate Frankie had this idea, this crazy, stupid idea. See, she watches *The Golden Girls* and…anyway, that doesn't matter. Basically, she thought I should have some fun by coming here and crashing the reunion. It was either this or online dating. Not that I have anything against online dating. I know a lot of people who've met significant others that way. But I just couldn't see any more penises."

Luke blinked, unsure which comment to jump on first. He decided to go with the easiest. "You didn't graduate with me?"

"Um, not unless you also didn't go to Kennedy High School."

"You didn't go to this school at all?"

"No, not technically."

"Are you even a librarian?"

"Yes, that's one hundred percent true. I'm a librarian here in Arlington. Frankie and I live in Shirlington. You know, the neighborhood in South Arlington."

"I know where Shirlington is. Cool area."

"Oh God, are you going to tell on us?"

"Depends. I have one more question for you." He'd made his voice as serious as he could. She waited, her eyes growing wide as apprehension spread across her face. "What's your real name?"

Her shoulders dropped in relief. "Lola. Lola McBride."

"Anything else I should know?"

"I'm twenty-six. I don't usually do things like this. I'm totally blind without my glasses, as you witnessed earlier." She took a deep breath. "I'm clean, neat, and I can bake a pretty good chocolate cake. I say I'm going to a body pump class at the gym sometimes, but really, I go to Target and buy a bunch of useless stuff from the dollar bins.

"I love to read, like seriously, more than anything in the world. My favorite book is *Wuthering Heights*, although I read every genre of fiction. Especially romance novels." She blushed. "I mean, not the super dirty ones." A wrinkle formed on her forehead. "Okay, I read the super dirty ones, too. I love them. Don't judge me. But I also donate to the local animal shelter. And I'm afraid of colonial people. I'm totally boring, really."

Luke didn't have the answers to the universe but he did know that boring was something that Lola McBride wasn't.

"Colonial people? Why are you afraid of them?"

"I don't know. They just freak me out. When you go to Mount Vernon, they talk to you. It wigs me out. Something about the buckles on their shoes."

He couldn't help it. He threw his head back and laughed.

She bit her lip. "And I'm still so, so sorry that I spilled Jell-O on you."

"It's just a shirt."

"Still. You must think I'm insane."

Quite the opposite. He hadn't met many women like her, and he was curious as hell. He was about to say so when his phone started vibrating again. He saw another text message. This one was from his sister, Gwen.

Mom said you are bringing a date to our reunion. True? False?

False. I'm not bringing anyone.

Oh well. I have this friend I'd love to fix you up with…

"Sorry. It's my crazy family. See we have this…"

Yet another text message popped up. This time it was from his third sister Winnie.

Hey, Gwen said she's setting you up with someone. But I have a coworker that would be perfect for you.

It was official—his family was driving him mad. Why

couldn't they just back off? It was bad enough that he was going to have to go to his family reunion next weekend, but to have this kind of pressure about a date…

That's when an idea started to form.

He eyed Lola. She was clutching her basket of Jane Austen books against her chest, looking nervous. Did she really think he cared that she'd lied and crashed his high school reunion? He actually thought it was pretty funny.

"I'm really sorry I lied to you," she said. She glanced down at the basket. "I know I'm taking this basket away from someone who actually went to school here and…"

"Here's the deal, Lola," he said, interrupting her. "I won't reveal your identity tonight. You can keep your Jane Austen basket and no one will be the wiser."

She blew out a sigh of relief. "Really? Ohmigod, you're amazing."

"But you have to do me a favor in return."

"Anything."

He flipped his phone over in his hands. "Come to my family reunion next weekend and be my pretend girlfriend."

• • •

Lola wasn't sure she'd heard him correctly.

Had the super-hot guy she'd been talking to just ask her to pretend to be his girlfriend? She must have misheard him. Not surprising, really. The whole night was a blur. From dressing up in this ridiculous outfit to practically being forced to talk to Luke to spilling Jell-O all over him, she was more than ready to say adios to her fake high school and hightail it back to her very real apartment where her comfy clothes lived.

But it was kinda hard when Luke's enticing chocolate-brown eyes were boring into hers. The guy really was some kind of Adonis. He was tall with an amazing body. Not to mention that cowboy-like face. He had strong cheekbones and a square jaw, complimented with just a touch of a light beard. His sandy blond hair was cut short and neat. He looked like a real-life Scott Eastwood, and that comparison was yum.

What in the world did he see in her?

The gym was applauding again. They must have read another raffle winner's name.

"What do you say?" Luke asked.

Okay, so he hadn't been kidding about his proposal.

"Let me get this right. You want me to pretend to be your girlfriend at your family's reunion?"

He nodded. "I know it sounds crazy, but you'd really be doing me a favor. Besides, it's only for one day."

Lola shuffled the basket of books from one arm to the other so she could wipe her palms against her borrowed dress. "You want me to lie."

The you've-gotta-be-kidding-me look he offered her brought Lola right back down to Earth. "Okay, so perhaps I've already been doing some lying. But, honestly, I'm not a liar by nature."

"Trust me, I can see that."

"And lying to your family on top of it. I mean, what if they find out?" Or worse, what if someone got hurt? Lola certainly knew how much a lie could cause pain.

Luke grinned, and Lola had to work extra hard to keep her legs strong so she didn't slide to the floor in a puddle of mush. Mush? More like lust.

"They won't find out," he said, confidence in his voice, his stance, his aura. Damn, that was appealing.

"Luke, don't get me wrong. I've enjoyed talking with you tonight and spilling an old-school dessert on you and stuff, but we don't know each other at all."

He nodded, as if her words made sense.

"Furthermore," she went on, "what if someone in your family asks for details or brings up something about you that I, as your pretend girlfriend, should know?" She snapped her fingers. "The jig will be up like that."

"I see your point. But…" he said, drawing out the word as he held a hand up, "there's a simple solution."

She started chewing on one of her recently polished fingernails, a nervous habit she despised. "There is?"

"Sure. I'm going to give you a crash course in all things Luke Erickson."

Lola couldn't help herself. She eyed him, starting from his feet, up his long, long legs, over that amazing body—with the stained shirt—and all the way to his insanely handsome face. He had the. Best. Lips. Period. She couldn't help but wonder what it would be like to kiss them.

Lick them.

Bite them.

"Hey, you okay? You're swaying," he said.

Yikes. Lola quickly pulled herself together. "Um, sorry. A little too much spinach and artichoke dip earlier. Must have been spiked, ha ha. Anyway, as much as I would um, enjoy, a crash course in you, I don't know that I have time this week."

"Come on, Lola. What about Monday night? No one ever does anything on Monday night. I'll buy you dinner. Anywhere you want."

"I play bocce on Monday nights."

Luke blinked. "Bocce? Did you just say bocce?"

She nodded. "Sure. Bocce is this Italian game where you throw different colored balls and try to get as close as you can to the—"

"I know what bocce is. Well, sort of. I wasn't aware that anyone under the age of seventy played it."

"Oh sure. A lot of people do. I'm in a bocce league."

He chuckled. He'd heard of softball leagues, soccer leagues, even kickball leagues. "There are bocce leagues? Are you serious?"

"As a heart attack. Well, we're kind of this rogue league. There's an actual league here in the D.C.-area that plays down on the National Mall, but they are soooo stuffy and serious. A bunch of us were fed up with the rules so we started our own league. We play over in this small park in Alexandria. They refurbished the park recently and put in a bocce court. It's near that Mexican restaurant. You know the one that has the patio seating with the light-up peppers?"

He shook his head. "I can't wrap my head around a bunch of girls playing bocce."

"Every Monday night."

"Let me get this straight. You're a high school reunion-crashing librarian who plays in a renegade bocce league and covets Jane Austen books?"

Was that strange? Coming out of his mouth it did seem kind of weird she supposed.

"Lola McBride, you keep getting more and more interesting by the second."

"Really?"

He stepped closer. "Really."

She wanted to acquiesce and go to his family reunion with him. But she was realizing that it was only to spend more time with him.

Her phone vibrated. Juggling the basket of books, she retrieved it from her purse. She glanced down and saw a text message from Frankie.

That guy is crazy hot. Go for it! #REBOUND

She put her phone in airplane mode. Then she looked up at Luke.

"I have a question. Why do you need to bring a girlfriend to your family reunion?"

"I have three sisters, who are triplets by the way. They've been pestering me since the day they were born."

Wow, three siblings. Jealousy traveled up Lola's spine at the thought of having sisters. Or siblings. Or anyone.

"The last couple of years the three of them, along with my wonderful, but very intrusive, mother have taken it upon themselves to badger me to death. They want me to settle down and start a family."

She noticed that he didn't mention a dad in this scenario. "What about your father?"

He shook his head. His gaze cast down to the floor.

"Sorry," she said. "I don't have a dad, either."

Or a mother. Or siblings, grandparents, or cousins. She should be used to it by now, but as usual, the thought made her want to cry. She gulped down a big breath and steadied herself. She'd had a mother and father, a very loving parental unit. Until the accident took her dad and cancer claimed her mom a couple years after that.

Not for the first time in her life, she wondered what it would be like to have a big, meddling family. Tons of people to spend holidays with, baking cookies and doing gift exchanges. Sunday dinners with lots of noise and food and laughter. Sure would beat Chinese takeout for one.

Any time one of her friends complained about their nosy family, she wanted to shake them. Didn't they see how lucky they were? Lola would give anything for a family, intrusive and interfering or not. But as usual, she knew she couldn't blurt that out to a stranger. Hell, she barely talked about it with Frankie.

"Can't you just tell your family to butt out?" she asked Luke.

Maybe she did want to spend more time with this hottie and get to know him better, but he was asking her to lie to his family. To his sisters and mother. The thought made her stomach roll. Crashing this reunion aside, Lola simply didn't condone lying. Even when it was coming from a good place, being untruthful caused damage. She knew that better than anyone.

"Asking wouldn't even make a dent with them." He laughed, but only for a moment before growing serious. "The truth is, I hate disappointing them. I don't want to settle down, but I also don't want to see that look of dissatisfaction on my mom's face when I walk through the door alone." He coughed into his fist, and his voice grew quieter. "My mom has done so much for me over the years."

True love and respect for his mother shone in his eyes, and that was her undoing. Even if going along with his plan went against her better judgment.

"Fine," she whispered.

"What was that?" Hope filled his eyes.

"I said okay, I'll do it."

"Yes! Lola, thank you so much. You will not regret this."

"I regret it already."

With that, he pulled her into a tight hug, crushing the basket of books as he did. He smelled amazing. Whatever kind of cologne he wore just about set her mouth watering. Not to mention the feel of his arms around her was amazing. She felt safe and cocooned.

Oh, she was definitely going to regret this.

She broke off the hug and took a large step backward. "Maybe we should exchange numbers."

Luke pulled out his phone. Just as Lola finished keying in her number, she heard a commotion. She turned in the direction of the sound as Frankie called her name, who was rushing toward her.

"Lola!" She waved as she hustled over.

"Frankie, hey, this is Luke. Luke, my roommate Frankie."

Luke shook Frankie's hand. "Ah, the orchestrator of

tonight's evil plot."

Lola sighed. "I honestly don't know why I'm friends with her at this point."

Luke leaned over and whispered softly, "I'm glad you are. We wouldn't have met otherwise."

Luke's words warmed her heart. She felt the struggle to keep from blushing. How many times had her cheeks reddened tonight?

Frankie nodded. "Speaking of my evil plot, we're busted."

Unused to getting in trouble for anything ever, Lola gasped. "What?"

"Our cover's blown. We gotta roll." Frankie turned to Luke. "Although, it was so nice to meet you." She batted her eyelashes in the most obvious way. Lola had to physically work from rolling her eyes. "I hope you had fun with my friend."

"It's definitely been enlightening. And I look forward to seeing your friend later this week."

"That's what I like to hear. Oh shit," Frankie said, eyeing the door they entered through earlier.

Lola and Luke both turned and saw one of the women who had been manning the table with the nametags, and she didn't look happy. Her hands were on her hips as she did a sweep of the gym. Frankie grabbed Lola's arm.

"Hold those books tights. Let's make a run for it. We can use that side door."

"Oh right." Lola smiled at Luke, who was already starting to laugh. "Um, bye Luke. See ya soon."

They made their way to the side of the gym and out the door into the humid June air. Even at night, the temperature was high and the humidity higher. It was going to be a hot summer in the D.C.-area.

An image of Luke flashed into her mind, and she bit her lip.

"I'll get us an Uber," Frankie said as they crossed the parking lot. "So…how was the hottie?"

"Great actually."

Frankie threw her fist into the air. "Victory. See, I told you all you had to do was follow *The Golden Girls* and you would be golden. Never doubt Dorothy, Rose, Blanche, and Sophia."

"Oh please." Lola was fighting the urge to remove her heels.

"You scoff and yet, I heard Hottie McHotterson say he would see you later this week. I smell a rebound fling."

Lola stopped, causing Frankie to pull up as well. "What?" Frankie asked.

"Luke is way more than simply a rebound fling." She paused dramatically, excited to watch Frankie's eyes bug out of her face.

"He's my rebound *boyfriend*."

Chapter Three

"Fasten your seatbelt, slut puppy. This ain't gonna be no cake walk!"
-Sophia Petrillo

"Lola has a rebound boyfriend. A super-secret rebound boyfriend," Frankie announced to their group of friends assembled for their weekly bocce game.

Lola sighed, even as the rest of her friends *oohed* and *aahed* and moved closer for more details. "It's just a secret from his family. Besides, it's not real," she said. "We're only pretending."

"That's why I said super-secret," Frankie said.

"Is he hot?" Katie asked.

"Ohmigod," Frankie said, fanning herself with her hand. "So effing hot. He looks like a movie star. Or a cowboy. Or a cowboy movie star. He's tall and built, and oh-so-yummy."

"Then why is he pretend?" Olivia wondered out loud. "Why don't you take the super-secret out of your relationship and just get with him?"

"Because I lied to him, and then he asked me to lie again. I hate lying."

Frankie sighed dramatically. "We all know your penchant for the truth. But honestly, Lola, we barely stretched the truth."

Lola snagged one of the light beers from their cooler bag, covertly popped the top, and poured it into a red solo cup. They weren't technically allowed to drink in this park, but what was a game of rogue bocce without some beer?

"I used a fake name."

"I always use a fake name when I meet guys in bars," Olivia said.

"This was different," Lola said. "We dressed up and pretended to be other people. In public."

"Huh?" Olivia asked.

"Frankie and I crashed Kennedy High's ten-year reunion on Saturday night." She filled them in on how she won the coveted Jane Austen basket and how she was supposed to attend his family reunion in exchange for his silence.

"That's awesome," Hannah said.

Katie jumped up. "They did that on an episode of *The Golden Girls*."

"Exactly," Frankie said emphatically. "Thank you."

"Frankie had this crazy idea that I needed to have a little rebound fling."

"Crazy?" Frankie huffed. "Um, hello, it worked. You met Luke, and now you have your rebound."

Lola rolled her eyes. "Whatever. The chance of me seeing Luke again is slim to none."

Celeste, who was the keeper of the balls for their bocce game, looked up from her crouched position on the ground where she was setting up the game. "What are you talking about? Didn't you just say you're going to his family reunion?"

Lola shook her head. "It's not like that's going to happen.

I'm sure he was just making conversation."

Frankie picked up one of the red balls. "We'll be Team Christmas this week," she said. That meant her team would throw the red and green balls. "You and Luke exchanged numbers."

"Right, but he's not going to call or anything. I mean, he didn't text me yesterday. More than likely he's forgotten all about it. He probably had one too many drinks that night."

Part of this statement was wishful thinking on Lola's part. She'd never done anything so impulsive as crashing a reunion before. To go a step further and pretend to be someone's girlfriend was insane, especially for someone she barely knew. No matter how hot he was.

And, man, was Luke Erickson hot. Against her will, she'd thought about him for the rest of the weekend and most of today. She adjusted her glasses and remembered his smile. It had almost brought her to her knees. Then there was his body. When she'd tried to help him clean up his shirt, her hands had paused on his rock-hard pecs. It had taken everything inside her not to continue feeling him up. But none of that mattered. She was more likely to crash another reunion than see Luke again.

"You really don't think you're going to hear from him?" Frankie asked.

"No," she said, exasperated. She loved Frankie, but the girl never let it go.

"Are you sure?"

She aimed a hard, no-nonsense stare in Frankie's direction. "Yes," she said through clenched teeth.

"What would you say to him if you did?"

Lola wanted to strangle her best friend. She stood up and faced her group of friends with one hand on her hip and the other holding onto her cup of beer. "What do you want me to say? The truth? Oh Luke, you're the hottest guy I've ever seen and I would absolutely love to pretend to be your girlfriend."

"Now that's what I like to hear."

Lola spun around so fast, her beer sloshed over the edge of the cup, dampening her light-blue tank top, and she almost fell over. When she saw Luke standing there looking like sex on a stick, she wished she had fallen—fallen into a deep, dark pit where she could hide for the rest of her life. She peeked over her shoulder at Frankie who seemed very pleased with herself. She winked at Lola.

Lola would kill her later.

"Ohmigod," she squeaked out. "Luke. Uh, what are you doing here?"

"You told me you and your friends play bocce here on Mondays, and I work not too far over in Old Town. But let's get back to that declaration you just made." He grinned.

Lola's cheeks felt like they were on fire.

"Hey, Luke," Frankie called. "Want a beer?"

"Sure," he replied. "I've never seen a rogue bocce game, so I thought I would come check it out. Actually, I've never seen a regular bocce game come to think of it." He accepted the red solo cup from Frankie. "Thanks. So how do you guys play?"

"It's super simple," Hannah said. "We throw out the pallina first."

"The what?" Luke asked.

"It's that little white ball," Katie said. "Then we start throwing the colored balls. Essentially, whoever gets closest to the pallina, wins."

"Seems simple enough," Luke said.

"It's harder than it looks, especially because our court is a little uneven. But that's part of the fun. So is the beer." Frankie tapped her cup to Luke's and smiled. "Want to play?"

"Good call," Celeste said. "Our friend Summer couldn't make it tonight, so the teams are uneven."

Did her friends really just ask hottie Luke to play bocce with them?

Lanette, who had been quiet until now, spoke up. "You can be part of Team Ikea with Katie, Celeste, and Lola, of course."

"Team Ikea?"

Olivia laughed. "Yeah, you guys are blue and yellow. Like Sweden."

"Like Ikea." Luke nodded. "Funny."

As they gathered up the balls and filled up their solo cups with beer, Frankie grabbed Lola's arm and whispered to her, "This is fabulous."

"It's awkward," Lola hissed back.

"What are you talking about? This is the perfect opportunity for you to bond with your pretend boyfriend. Show him how you work the balls." She wiggled her eyebrows.

Lola shoved her friend. "You're disgusting."

"But you love me anyway." With that, Frankie made her way toward her team.

Lola sighed and grabbed two balls from the ground. She crossed to Luke. "Here are your blue balls."

She froze. *Kill me now.* She did not just say that. Lola closed her eyes tight and wished for a major do-over. But the sound of Luke's husky laughter brought her right back to reality. She peeked through her lids, but she was still standing in the middle of the bocce court.

"You continue to amuse me, Lola McBride."

He put his arm around her shoulders, allowing her to take in his amazing cologne. Together, they joined the rest of the rogue league. Blue balls and all.

• • •

Who would have thought that an evening spent drinking

cheap beer and playing bocce with a bunch of girls would be so fun? But Luke was thoroughly enjoying himself.

Turned out he wasn't half bad at bocce, either. Although Team Christmas still ended up with the win.

Lola's friends were really funny and a blast to hang out with. He knew several of his friends would have loved the opportunity to hang out with seven gorgeous women. He was certainly relishing it.

Then there was Lola.

He glanced over at her. She had her head tilted back as she laughed at something Frankie said. Her smile lit up her entire face. A soft breeze blew her long brown hair around her shoulders.

She'd been nervous earlier. It was adorable. But after the first couple bocce throws—not to mention some beer— she'd calmed down. When she did, he learned that she was extremely funny. And bright. And down to earth. And sexy.

Ah hell. He was starting to like her. Not good. He needed to put the kibosh on any feelings, because he simply wasn't interested in a relationship. Besides, they had a whole ruse to think about. Falling for his pretend girlfriend was way more complicated than he needed things to get.

"Well, I guess I should be going," Frankie announced rather dramatically.

"Going home?" Lola asked. "What about ice cream?"

"Ice cream?" Luke looked from Lola to Frankie. The other girls were dispersing, offering their congrats to Team Christmas and saying goodbyes until next week.

"Yeah," Lola said. "Frankie and I always get ice cream after bocce. It's our tradition."

"Beer and ice cream. Hmm. Not my first choice in combos," he said.

"Sorry, Lo. I, uh, have a thing."

Lola put her hands on her hips. "What thing? It's almost

eight at night."

Frankie scrunched her nose. "Exactly. My thing is really early tomorrow morning." She let out a very loud and fake yawn. "I need to get to bed. Sorry to miss out on the ice cream. Oh wait, I know." Frankie gestured as if she'd just received the answer to the world's greatest question. "Why doesn't Luke take you for ice cream?"

Luke stifled his laughter. Frankie was quite the character and watching her ruffle Lola's serious feathers was beyond amusing. In terms of personalities, they were definitely the odd couple of roommates.

"I could go for some ice cream," Luke said.

"Did someone say ice cream?" Olivia asked as she swung her backpack on her back. "I'd love some—arghhh," she finished when Frankie hit her in the stomach. The two of them exchanged meaningful glances. Finally, Olivia nodded. "I mean, I'm lactose intolerant. That's why I'd like ice cream. Always. But I can't have any because, you know, my lactose problems. Well, Frankie, let's get going."

"I've literally never seen the two of them move so fast in my life," Lola said as they watched Frankie and Olivia's retreating backs. "They're ridiculous."

"They're hysterical. All of your friends are. I had fun tonight."

"I'm glad. And listen, you don't have to get ice cream if you don't want."

"Pass up thick milky goodness after all that lite beer? Are you crazy?"

She eyed him for a moment, probably weighing if he was teasing her or not. Finally, she said, "Okay then, follow me. There's a great parlor down the street."

They walked a short distance to a hole-in-the-wall place with a long counter and room for only one tiny table and two café-style chairs. Luke didn't expect much, but when he started perusing the glass display cases under the counter, he realized the little ice cream parlor had some weight. All of the usual flavors were there, but half of the offerings were for unique pairings like lavender honey, basil, and even a maple syrup mix.

The line moved quickly, and when it was their turn, Luke ordered a waffle cone with chocolate marshmallow. He stepped to the cashier. "And please add on whatever the lady is ordering."

"Thanks, Luke." Lola smiled. "Vanilla in a sugar cone please."

Luke shook his head and paid for the two cones. Then they made their way outside to a bench.

"Vanilla? Seriously? All of those flavors and you get vanilla?"

She shrugged and turned her nose up at him.

"Plain Jane vanilla. You didn't even add any toppings. No sprinkles. No chocolate chips. No syrup."

"Maybe I don't need anything extra to enjoy my vanilla ice cream. My ice cream happens to be delicious and refreshing." She poked him the chest. "Not everything has to be sparkly and glittery, and unique and different, you know. Some things are amazing just as they are."

He took her in as she defended her boring ice cream. She'd pulled her hair back in a ponytail while they walked to the ice cream shop. She was wearing jean shorts, a baby-blue tank top, and plain white sneakers. Her face was scrubbed clean of makeup, and the only jewelry she had on were tiny hoop earrings and a delicate silver chain with a small circle charm. There was nothing fancy about her. Yet, she took his breath away.

"I think I see your point," he said on an unsteady breath.

"How's yours?" She nodded at his cone.

"Really good. Want to try some?"

"Duh. It's chocolate."

He couldn't remember the last time he sat outside an ice cream shop and enjoyed a cone. His dad used to take him and his sisters every Friday night. One of them would always spill their ice cream. Then they would start to cry. But Luke's dad would laugh and simply buy them a new cone. After, they'd walk through this park that was near their house, and their dad would push them on the swings. Luke used to get so high on the swing he felt as if he were flying.

He almost gasped at the unwelcome memory. It was rare for him to have thoughts of his dad. In fact, he worked hard to keep his old man out of his mind. Then he saw Lola take a big lick of his ice cream and all thoughts—of his dad or anything else in the world—simply disappeared. She lapped at the chocolate, her tongue devouring the ice cream in one fluid motion. Her eyes fluttered shut as a sensuous moan escaped her lips. She delicately dabbed at the corner of her mouth with her finger before licking that as well.

Luke didn't move. He didn't breathe. He didn't think.

"Mmm, so good," she whispered.

The sound of her voice shot straight to his groin, and suddenly his pants were feeling snug. He could have dumped every tub of ice cream in the joint on top of his head and still felt overheated.

Lola's eyes opened, and she trained her gaze on his face; she cocked her head. "Are you okay?"

I want you. "Uh, yeah, I'm fine. Why?"

"Because you're breathing really hard. Do you have asthma?"

Shit. She was so damn perceptive. Thank God she wasn't also a mind reader, because the thoughts running through his would definitely drive her away.

"Um, no asthma. I have allergies though."

Everyone in the D.C.-area had allergies. The place was

notorious for it.

Lola nodded as if his explanation cleared up everything. "The pollen is really bad this week."

They sat in silence for a while, enjoying their ice cream and people watching. The setting sun had helped cool down the sweltering June temperature, and there were lots of people taking advantage of it. Dogs were being walked, parents were pushing babies in strollers, and kids were running around in the park. Some with ice cream-stained faces, Luke noted.

When Lola finished her boring ice cream cone, she turned to Luke. "So do you still want to do this whole family reunion thing this weekend?"

He took the last bite of his cone and threw his napkin away. "You mean, do I still want you to pretend to be my girlfriend?"

She bit her lip and a light-red blush colored her cheeks. "Yeah."

"Of course. Did you think I forgot about it?"

She tugged on her ponytail. "More like, I hoped you'd forget about it."

Luke couldn't resist. He ran his fingers through her shiny hair and also gave a little yank on her ponytail. "No such luck. Although, I'm not going to force you to do anything, especially if you're uncomfortable with it."

She was quiet for a long moment. Luke could tell she was deeply considering what he'd said. "No, I made you a promise. I'll be there. Besides, I don't want you to turn me in for taking the Jane Austen basket the other night."

He leaned toward her and lowered his voice conspiratorially. "I was never going to turn you in for that."

"Really?" she squeaked.

"Really. I thought it was funny."

"I promised to come to your family reunion for nothing."

"Pretty much."

She nodded solemnly. "So who will I be meeting this weekend?" she asked.

"My mom Lorraine and my Aunt Sally. A bunch of cousins will be there, too. Plus, you'll meet my three sisters. I think I told you they're triplets. Mia, Winnie, and Gwen."

"Wow, I've never met triplets before. Are they identical?"

"No, thank God. They are a handful as is. I can't imagine if they had the power to switch places on us. It would have been extreme pandemonium growing up."

"How old are they?"

"They're twenty-seven, a year younger than me."

"Are you guys close?"

He felt his phone vibrate in his pocket. No doubt it was one of his sisters. *Pains in the butt that they are*, he thought with a grin. "Yeah, we're pretty close. They're ecstatic that I moved back to the area. Gives them even more ways to annoy me."

She smiled, but it didn't last long. A shadow passed over her face. Even behind her glasses, he could tell that her eyes had turned a deeper, darker blue.

Luke replayed their conversation and tried to figure out what could have bothered her, but he came up at a loss. He was about to ask when she spoke up.

"You said you moved back here. Where were you?"

"Guess," he said.

A curious smile spread across her face. "You were being a cowboy on a ranch in New Mexico. A super hot ranch. And bandits tried to rob it of cattle or whatever, but you stopped them."

Again, Luke wasn't sure what he'd expected her to say, but that definitely wasn't it. "Um, nope. I wasn't on a ranch."

"You weren't being a cowboy?" She sounded disappointed.

"Sorry, no. I don't even know how to ride a horse. I lived

in San Francisco and then Manhattan."

"Wow. How cool. Which city did you like better?"

He considered her question. Lately, it seemed like his family only cared about the fact that he'd returned and never asked about his actual time there.

"I loved both of them. San Fran is unique. No place like it. And then there was New York. It was frenetic and fast-paced. So many interesting people and great restaurants. I don't know if I could live there forever, but I'm really glad I did for a couple years."

They continued talking about different cities they'd been to as people went in and out of the ice cream shop. Lola hadn't been to a ton of places, but those she had visited clearly left a big impression.

"I have to wonder about you."

"Oh yeah?" he asked in an amused voice.

"Yeah. You're successful and well-traveled and funny. Plus, you're…good looking." She blushed again. Damn, he loved when she did that.

"I believe you already said I was the hottest guy you've ever seen."

"Yeah, I totally knew you were standing behind me when I said that." She laughed awkwardly. "But seriously, I would imagine you could get a date to your family reunion like that." She snapped her fingers next to her face.

"Probably, but my family doesn't want me to bring any old date. They want me to be in a relationship."

"And this would be a problem for you?"

"I'm not exactly the world's biggest fan of relationships."

"Really? Why?"

Because of my dad. The thought came and went so quickly he was almost shocked by it. Unfortunately, it was true.

Luke had been five and his sisters only four when his father announced at the dinner table that he was leaving.

Luke hadn't understood. He thought maybe his dad was running out to the store or going back to work, but his mom had started crying, which made him and all of his sisters do the same.

The next thing he knew, his grandmother and aunts had come over. His mother stayed in her bedroom for an entire week. Eventually, she returned to her job as a nurse. But his dad never returned to their house, to their family.

The first couple of years, he would send cards with money in them for their birthdays and holidays. Then the cards stopped as well. His dad signed full custody over to his mom, and Luke hadn't seen him since.

He didn't want to see him.

"Luke?" Lola's voice pulled him out of his mind and back to reality. She was staring at him with curiosity.

"Sorry."

"Where'd you go?"

"Just thinking about your question. I guess I'm not into relationships because I don't see them working."

"Ever?" she asked on a half laugh.

He shrugged. A piece of paper—legal or otherwise—wasn't able to stop his dad from going his own way. "It's rare. Most don't last very long. Someone gets bored and leaves. It's human nature, I guess."

"Does your family know you feel this way?" she asked.

He nodded. "I've mentioned it once or twice or a million times."

"Then why bring someone—real or pretend—to this reunion at all?"

It was a fair question. He tried to answer honestly. "I had an excuse not to go to our reunions all those years I lived out of state. But since I moved back to the area recently, they've been driving me nuts about settling down, no matter how many times I tell them it's never gonna happen," he said when

Lola started to protest. "I thought if they could see me with someone one time, they might lay off for a while. Bother one of my sisters or cousins about something for a change."

"What about after the reunion?" she asked.

Luke had already considered this point. "Afterwards, we'll fake break up. Then my family will feel bad for me, which will buy even more time for them to lay off me. Give me a little reprieve."

"Well, I'm not really onboard with your logic. I don't approve of lying, especially to your family. Lies have a way of hurting. Trust me."

"It's only a small lie." He was rationalizing, and he knew it. Still, bringing someone to meet his family would save him from a million headaches. "Telling my mom and sisters that we're together is a little fib that has no possibility of hurting anyone."

She removed her glasses and rubbed her eyes. "When you're masking the truth, there's always a way that it can backfire. Trust me."

Her eyes filled with sadness. Luke had to wonder why she was so averse to lying. Who had hurt her? Who'd lied to her? "Lola—"

She shook her head and put her glasses back on. "I'll still help you anyway."

She reached over and squeezed his hand. As soon as her fingers touched his, it felt like a bolt of lightning shot through him. Awareness and heat and something much more primal bubbled to the surface.

"I'll be your reprieve," she said.

Luke could barely talk. She was still holding his hand, and whatever feeling her touch had incited, it was still coursing through him.

If anything, he knew that pretending Lola McBride was his girlfriend would be anything but a reprieve.

Chapter Four

"Go to sleep, sweetheart. Pray for brains."
-Dorothy Zbornak

After Luke had walked Lola back to her car the night before, they'd made plans for Wednesday night. They were going to order food and do a round of lets-get-to-know-each-other-real-fast.

That was Lola's idea. She said in order to pull off their pretend relationship they needed to know details, likes and dislikes, favorite things, and more. She insisted there would be a need for a master list and organization.

Luke was just looking forward to seeing her again. If he had to make a list to do so, well, that's what he'd do.

All morning he kept thinking about her. She'd looked so beautiful the night before. He liked talking to her. He liked the way she licked his ice cream. Yeah, he really liked that.

He shook his head and *tsked*. He'd gotten nothing accomplished all morning. Not to mention, that he really needed to curb all the liking he was doing with Lola. As great as she seemed so far, he simply didn't do relationships. He may not know all her likes and dislikes and favorites yet, but he knew enough to realize that Lola McBride was a relationship-type of girl.

Right now, he needed to be cognizant of keeping their relationship in the pretend-only category. Yet, when his boss asked if anyone wanted to join him in South Arlington for a quick meeting with a client, Luke jumped up. Lola worked at the Shirlington Library, only a couple blocks from where they were going to be. He could surprise her.

An hour and a half later, Luke left the meeting feeling optimistic about work and excited about his personal life. He headed over to the library. It wasn't the largest library, but it did sit right in the heart of the Shirlington neighborhood, in South Arlington. A neighborhood that boasted dozens of restaurants and bars, a large dog park, tons of bike and walking trails, and easy access into D.C. or Old Town Alexandria.

Lola said she and Frankie lived in an apartment in Shirlington. He wondered which one. There were apartments, condos, and townhouses galore.

He entered the library, taking a moment to relish the blast of air conditioning. It was another ninety-plus day in the nation's capital. D.C. was known for its hot and humid summers, but June wasn't usually quite this bad.

He took a few steps into the library. His gaze swept the rows of computers and comfortable recliners up against the wall of windows. People were busy typing away and perusing books and magazines. He could hear some kids over in the corner of the room. No doubt it was the children's corner.

He sauntered up to the counter where two women were working. "Excuse me, can you tell me if Lola McBride is working today?"

One of the women—her nametag identified her as

Sandy—pointed toward an area behind a couple of large printers. "Lola is helping a customer right now. She should be finished shortly."

The other woman, whose nametag was obscured by her long hair, said, "Lola didn't tell us she was expecting a visitor today."

"Yeah, well, this was a spur of the moment thing. I wanted to surprise her."

"How sweet," Sandy said.

"It is sweet." The second woman nodded in agreement. "So, you're one of Lola's, um, friends?"

Luke had to bite his cheek to keep from laughing at the overly obvious fishing. Sandy elbowed her coworker in the ribs.

The other woman rolled her eyes and then glanced at her watch. "Lola's due for her lunch break soon."

Perfect. "Thanks," Luke said and crossed the room.

He found Lola talking to an older man. Luke leaned against a stack and watched Lola in her element. She was patiently explaining something, and the man was nodding and taking notes.

She was wearing a navy-blue pencil skirt—a fashion term he'd overheard his sisters using—and a cream-colored tank top. The outfit was demure and professional, yet sexy as hell. When she reached for a book on a top shelf, she went on tiptoes and her shirt rode up, revealing just the briefest hint of smooth, silky skin.

Luke almost swallowed his tongue.

She continued speaking with the older gentleman, pointing out things and using her hands to gesture around the library. She walked him toward the copier and must have been instructing him on how to use it. She removed her glasses and dusted the lenses off with the edge of her top.

Those damn glasses, Luke thought. Why did they make

him respond this way? If there was no one else in the library, he'd like to take her behind the stacks and have his way with—

"Luke?"

He snapped to attention at Lola's voice. "Uh, hi, Lola."

"What are you doing here?"

"I had a meeting not far from here. I thought I would stop by and see if you wanted to grab lunch."

"Lunch?" Her cheeks reddened.

"Yeah, lunch is typically the middle meal of the day. People eat it anywhere between noon and two."

She batted at his shoulder. "You're so clever. Maybe you should be working in the library instead of me."

"Oh no, trust me. You look wayyyy better here than I…I mean, I think you're right where you should be."

She offered him a quizzical look but didn't say anything to his slipup. She started walking toward the info desk at the front of the library. He dutifully followed her. "It's actually time for my lunch break. Did you have a place in mind? There're lots of options around here."

"Nope, nothing specific," he said.

She checked in with her coworkers and then grabbed her purse. Luke couldn't help but see the two women grin at Lola. One of them even winked.

They headed out into the heat, and Lola stopped and tilted her face up to the sun. "Mmm, feels good."

Why did every sound she made sound so sexual? Luke hadn't been with a woman in a couple months, but he usually had more restraint than this.

"I've been cooped up in the air conditioning all day. This feels great." She ran a hand down the column of her neck. Then she shook her hair back over her shoulder. "What are you in the mood for?"

You. Naked. On the info desk.

Luke shook his head. "You pick. You know this area

better than me. Last time I lived here, there was hardly anything in this neighborhood."

"It really has changed. They've built Arlington up so much over the last decade." She peered down the street. "How about…pizza?"

Luke was impressed. He fully expected her to want some boring salad with dressing on the side. But she surprised him yet again. Lola showed him to a pizzeria. As soon as they entered the place, the aroma of tomato sauce, oregano, and cheese wafted out to greet him. His mouth watered immediately.

Lola suggested they split a pizza and take it to go. "Let's eat outside."

"You do realize it's over ninety degrees today."

She laughed. "Afraid you'll melt? Don't worry. I know a nice, shady spot by some water."

After their pie with pepperoni, extra cheese, and mushrooms was ready, they grabbed two waters and headed back through the main street of Shirlington. They crossed the street and walked over a little wooden bridge and found a bench.

"What is this place?" he asked.

"This," she said, sweeping her arm toward a long black fence surrounded by trees on one side and a bubbling stream on the other, "is the Shirlington Dog Park. It's a quarter-mile area for dogs to run and play. See, sometimes the dogs go down and play in the stream." She pointed toward a couple of labs happily splashing in the water.

Lola was right about the shady spot and the pizza. Both were great. When he took his last bite, he wiped his mouth with a napkin and leaned back on the park bench. "This really hit the spot."

From their dark-green bench they had a prime view of the dogs running around, enjoying their off-leash time. Lola sighed as she watched a couple of the dogs chase a ball. "I really want one."

He'd like one, too. "What's stopping you?"

"My landlord. Frankie and I rent, and there's a no-pet clause. Plus, Frankie's allergic anyway. But someday…it would be nice to have someone."

Someone? Luke's curiosity piqued.

"What about your family?" Luke realized they'd only talked about his family last night. He didn't even know if she had any siblings. "Do they live around here?"

She shook her head, but her eyes stayed trained on the ground in front of them. She curled one leg under her and then smoothed her skirt over her knee.

"So you're another D.C.-transplant, huh?" The D.C.-area was so transient. Between all of the colleges, the insecurity of jobs on the Hill, the military, people were always coming and going in the nation's capital.

"Actually, I'm from Alexandria."

Oh. "Did your parents move out of the area?"

"They died."

Yikes. His stomach clenched, the pizza forming a big old knot. "Both of them?"

"Yeah. My dad died in a car accident when I was in high school, and my mom had cancer. It came on really fast. Well, um, sort of."

Sort of? What did that mean?

"She died when I was in college."

Lola said the words robotically, like she had repeated them a thousand times. But the look in her eyes belied the stoicism in her voice.

"I'm really sorry."

She shrugged.

He wasn't sure how to proceed. "What about other family?"

She shook her head and glanced down. "Nope."

"What do you mean nope?"

"I don't have any family. I don't have any siblings. Both my parents were only children so I don't have aunts, uncles, or cousins either."

His heart ached for her. "I'm so sorry, Lola. That must be hard." She had to feel so alone. He took a gulp from his bottle of water. It did nothing to help with the large ball that formed there.

"Oh, it's fine. I mean, it's not *really* fine, but I'm used to it by now."

But if her body language was telling, she wasn't used to it. Then again, could a person ever really get used to losing both parents at such a young age?

"It's one of the reasons I'm so close to Frankie. We went to college together and decided to room together after. She's like my family now. No matter how many episodes of *The Golden Girls* she makes me watch or how many insane ideas she comes up with."

"Well, I'm glad she came up with the crazy idea of you crashing a reunion. If she didn't, we would have never met."

That brought a smile back to her face. "I don't know. You might rethink that statement after this weekend."

"Something tells me we're going to have a great weekend. And, hey, if it's really, truly awful, we'll just slip out the back door and go see a movie."

She giggled. "That's how my parents met."

"Oh yeah?"

She nodded. "Kinda. My dad had been set up with this woman who was apparently awful. He went out on a big group date with a bunch of friends. His date started making out with one of his friends. He was so annoyed that he slipped out of the theater and ducked into a different movie. My mom had bought a ticket for some romantic comedy, but she went into the wrong theater."

"Let me guess. She ran into your dad?"

Lola grinned and pointed at him. "You got it. They sat a couple seats away from each other. Turns out the movie was really scary. My mom kept inching closer and closer to my dad. The rest is…history."

She'd seemed alive and happy while she told the story. As soon as she finished, Luke noticed that that spark went out. Sadness replaced it. How horrible to lose both parents so young. And to not have any siblings or cousins or anything. Since he had about a million cousins, it was hard for him to comprehend. His family drove him crazy, but at least they were around to drive him crazy.

He didn't like that her face had fallen and that her eyes held such melancholy. He wanted to see her happy again. Without thinking, he cupped her cheek. He meant to comfort her. Only, he didn't know what words to use. What in the world could he ever say to make her situation better?

Behind those sexy glasses, Lola's eyes met his. Unshed tears pooled in them. He brought his other hand up so that he was framing her face. Then he gently brought his lips to hers. A surprised little gasp escaped her lips. But then she softened. Her eyes fluttered shut, and her lips molded to his.

The kiss was sweet and light, yet the feel of her lips on his was intoxicating. His breath caught even as the kiss went deeper. He tasted the tang of the pizza sauce and the spice from the pepperoni.

This close to her, he could smell her perfume. It was something delicate and floral. Very feminine and very potent.

Their mouths were fused, and their lips moved together in perfect harmony. While the kiss had begun so sweetly, it was quickly becoming more. Much more.

He'd kissed tons of women in his life, but none of them had ever felt like this. He didn't want it to end. For the next several minutes—or hours, he had no idea—it didn't.

Finally, they parted and for one split second, they exchanged a glance that was pregnant with wonder and lust and curiosity. He really hadn't meant to do that. All he'd meant to do was…

He ran a hand over his jaw. What? What had his intentions been? To comfort someone who'd lost both of her parents, sure. But there was more, and he would be lying if he denied it.

Lola was watching him intently, her chest rising and falling. He couldn't stop it, his gaze drifted down. There was something about the conservatively dressed librarian panting on a park bench after having been kissed thoroughly that made him want to yell out in triumph. More, he wanted to throw her over his shoulder and—

"Luke?" she asked shyly.

"Sorry, what?"

"I asked if you were okay. Your face is all red."

Was it? He could blame the heat, but he wouldn't. He didn't regret what had just transpired between them. Yet, he wasn't sure it had been the right thing to do.

"I, uh…"

He didn't get to finish the thought. Thank God. He didn't know what to say. He heard a loud bark, followed by more barking and *woofs* and *arfs*. Then Lola scooted back on the bench and gasped.

"Oh no." Her hand flew to her mouth as if she was in shock.

Shit. He'd definitely taken it too far. Women like Lola didn't make out in the middle of the day in a public place. "Look, Lola, I'm sorry about that. I should have asked you before I planted my lips on yours."

She dropped her hand. "How did that happen?"

Did he tell her the truth? That she was smokin' hot

and he'd wanted to kiss her since he'd first seen her in that tight dress last Saturday? He opened his mouth to attempt some kind of polite explanation just as a herd of dogs came charging by the bench.

"They got loose," a harried man screamed as several people chased after the pack of dogs, happily running freely.

Both he and Lola popped up. Pandemonium ensued. Dogs were running, owners were screaming, kids were laughing. A barrage of dog names and commands were being shouted.

"Koda, get back here!"

"No, no, Harry, don't follow Koda."

"Mr. Bigglesworth, Ms. Tuftsy, come back."

"Heel, Koda, heel."

"Who left the gate open?"

"Help!" someone called as they ran by him and Lola.

With no time to waste, Lola and Luke tried to do what they could to help. They managed to round up an overweight Shih Tzu named Ms. Tuftsy and an adorable poodle mix named Harry, who immediately started smelling Ms. Tuftsy's behind. The culprit of the dog park breakout appeared to be a small black lab named Koda, who broke free only to chase a couple of squirrels up a tree, jumping and barking happily and completely oblivious to the havoc she'd incited.

As the chaos calmed down, Luke turned to Lola. They both started laughing.

"Well," he began.

"Well."

"That was an eventful lunch. Is it always like this in Shirlington?"

She grinned. "Maybe not quite as exciting."

Luke decided he should try one more time to talk about what had happened on the bench. "Listen, I just want to say…"

"Ohmigod," Lola screeched. She'd glanced at her watch. "Oh no. I'm late. I gotta get back to work."

They booked it back to the library and said a quick goodbye. There was no time to talk about the kiss that had just happened.

That was a good thing, Luke thought. Because with a kiss like that, he truly had no words.

Chapter Five

"My first was Billy. Oh, I'll never forget it! That night under the dogwood tree, the air thick with perfume, and me with Billy. Or Bobby? Yes, that's right, Bobby! Or was it Ben? Oh who knows, anyway, it started with a B."
-Blanche Devereaux

"Who's ready for a little more smooching?"

Lola turned from her closet where she was weighing her outfit options. The confident look on Frankie's face did nothing to assuage the nerves fluttering around in her belly over her impending night with Luke. She threw a shoe at her roommate.

Frankie caught the heel and grinned. "Are you nervous about tonight, Lola McBride?"

"No." Lola pulled out a green sundress, studied it, and then quickly returned it to the closet. "Yes. I am. Help me."

She collapsed onto her bed, and Frankie followed her. "What am I supposed to wear to a session of getting to know my pretend boyfriend? I've never had to dress for something like this before."

Frankie tilted her head. "Hmm, maybe the real question is what do you wear to see Luke who you kissed yesterday afternoon? A very real kiss with your very pretend boyfriend." For extra emphasis, Frankie batted her eyelashes dramatically.

"I knew I would regret telling you about that kiss."

"Hey, I wouldn't be commenting on it if nothing had happened. You're the one who smooched, and I'm the one who gets the details."

"I'm going to stop telling you things about my life," Lola said. She tried to put conviction into her voice even though she couldn't imagine ever following up on the threat. Not spilling her guts to Frankie every day would be like not brushing her teeth.

"Oh please. I'm your bestie."

"For some unknown reason." Lola shoved Frankie's shoulder lightly, but Frankie simply grinned.

"Pretend to hate me all you want, but I know you better than that. You're trying to divert attention because what you really want is to play mouth-capades with Luke again."

Frankie hit the nail on the head. That kiss had been… unexpected. A total surprise, and yet, completely and utterly satisfying. The only bad thing about it was that it had ended. She couldn't help but wonder what would have happened if the kiss hadn't ended. She'd probably have done something truly indecent on that park bench, where anyone could see them.

Maybe the intrusion was a good thing after all.

"It's just awkward, you know?" she said to Frankie, who nodded her head in total understanding. "Luke kissed me, I'm not even really sure why, and then the dogs got loose. Then I had to run back to work so I wasn't late."

Frankie crossed to Lola's closet and started riffling

through it. She pulled out a cute pink tank with white polka dots.

"What do you mean you aren't sure why he kissed you?"

Lola got comfortable on the bed. "Just that. We were having lunch and talking, and then I told him about my parents—"

Frankie stopped in the middle of deciding between two pairs of Lola's sandals. Her head snapped up. "Whoa. You told Luke about your parents?"

Lola shrugged. "It's not like it's a secret."

"I know. It's just, you don't usually bring them up so soon after meeting someone."

Again, Lola shrugged. She couldn't think of a gesture better fit for the situation. "It felt natural. Next thing I know, Luke cupped my face—"

Frankie sighed. "I love when they cup our faces."

"Me too," Lola said. "Then his lips were on mine."

Frankie handed the pink tank and a pair of cute white sandals to Lola, who accepted them gratefully. "Wear this with simple jean shorts. You're just going to his place. No need to waste one of your super-cute outfits. You want to go for casual mixed with a hint of hotness."

"Got it. But, Frankie, why do you think he kissed me?"

Frankie rolled her eyes as she flopped down onto Lola's bed. "Because he's a guy. Because you're gorgeous. Because he likes you. Who cares really? This isn't one of life's biggest mysteries, Lo. Just enjoy it."

"Should I bring it up tonight?"

"And say what? Remember that time yesterday when you kissed me after we had pepperoni pizza? Just be natural."

"I was natural with Mark."

Frankie's eyes softened. "I know you were. But for what it's worth, I never liked Mark. Even before he dumped you."

Lola bit her lip. "You mean, before he dumped me for

that young twenty-two-year-old."

"Oh geez, Lola. You sound like you're an old spinster. You're only twenty-six. And anyway, Mark was too..." Frankie pressed a finger to her mouth as she considered.

"Too serious?" Lola supplied. "Too reserved?"

Frankie thrust her finger into the air. "Too much of a dick."

Lola burst into laughter, and her friend joined her. She loved these moments with Frankie. Laughing until their bellies hurt. When they were roommates in college, they'd stayed up the whole first night talking. Frankie had her in hysterics. She knew from that moment that they'd be friends for life.

After a few more moments of giggling, they settled down. Lola couldn't help it; she grew pensive again.

"Luke doesn't do relationships. He doesn't want a girlfriend. This is all pretend. For real. Some guys say no relationships, but I think this guy like literally means it."

Frankie bit her lip. "Do you want it to be more than pretend?"

She shrugged, trying to appear nonchalant when really she felt anything but. Almost everything she knew about Luke so far turned her on. He was attractive and funny. He rolled with the punches and fit in well with her friends. He was decent at bocce, and man could he kiss.

The only thing that bugged her was the lying factor. It really rubbed her the wrong way that he could so easily fool his family.

"It's something to keep in mind while we're faking this relationship."

Frankie stayed silent for a moment. A very long moment, which was unusual for her typical chatty friend. Finally, she said, "Yes, it is." She tapped Lola's heart. "It's important to protect this."

The mood had turned solemn, and it was unsettling for Lola. She tried to lighten it. "I thought you wanted me to have fun."

"Oh, I do. So long as you can remember to *only* have fun with Luke. Nothing more."

"Don't worry, Frankie. I can do that."

The problem was that Lola didn't know if she could follow up on that promise. Luke may be lying to his family, but she'd just lied to her best friend. She didn't know if she could keep herself from falling for Luke.

. . .

Luke stared at his phone and shook his head. He needed a drink.

He'd officially told his mom and sisters that he was dating someone and that he would be bringing his new girlfriend to the family reunion on Saturday.

This announcement was followed by an insane amount of text messages that contained more exclamation points than he'd ever seen in his entire life. Winnie shot him a bitmoji that featured her avatar pumping her fists into the air. Mia sent him a text with fireworks bursting in the background. He wasn't sure what his mother tried to say, because it had been autocorrected.

Only his sister Gwen seemed less than enthused. In fact, her response was concise and filled with suspicion.

A new girlfriend? And right before the family reunion. How convenient.

Gwen always was the cynical one. And the perceptive one. And the one who was usually right.

Shit.

He and Lola would have to stay on their toes around her. Speaking of Lola, she was due at his place any minute. They were going to spend the evening getting to know each other on a couple's level.

Luke didn't know if their kiss the other day would make that harder or easier. All he knew was that he hadn't stopped thinking about it since.

The sexy librarian kissed like a dream. It was too good to be true.

Still, Luke wasn't interested in a relationship. Even though he didn't know her that well yet, he knew enough to realize that Lola McBride was a relationship kind of girl. Nothing wrong with that. It's just that he shouldn't have kissed her.

He wanted to kiss her again.

Damn. Luke tried to run a hand through his hair until he remembered that he'd recently chopped it all off.

He needed to remind himself that this wasn't a real date. He'd just met Lola not even a week earlier. Plus, he had been honest with her about his feelings on relationships.

But had he been honest with himself?

He shook his head and glanced around his condo. Okay, so maybe he had cleaned up the place a bit in anticipation of his fake girlfriend coming over. And he'd lit a couple candles. So what? They always did that in those design shows his sister Winnie forced him to watch.

It created ambiance. There was nothing wrong with that.

And there had been nothing wrong with that kiss yesterday either. But should he mention it tonight? Would she? What if she did and wanted to like, talk about it in depth?

Better yet, what if she wanted to repeat it? That would be much more preferable to talking.

There was a knock on his door, and he immediately glanced in the closest mirror. He ran a hand over his recently shaved jawline.

What was he doing? This wasn't a real date.

He yanked the door open, and his mouth immediately

watered. Lola stood there looking like sex on a stick in short jean shorts and an, um, flattering, tank top. Very flattering. It showcased all of her curves.

"Hi," she said shyly.

"Hey, Lola, come on in." His voice came out huskier than he would have liked. But he ignored that and ushered Lola inside.

"Great place," she said, setting her bag down and taking a small lap around his condo.

It was a newer building that had been constructed in the last year. Just in time for him to move back to Arlington. It boasted two bedrooms, two baths, a killer balcony that would have a view of the fireworks over the Washington Monument on the Fourth of July. He had granite countertops, all new appliances, and dark laminate floors.

"It's so grown-uppy," Lola said. "Kind of puts my apartment to shame."

Lola lived in South Arlington where the buildings tended to be older than here in North Arlington. Luke was glad he'd bought the place and loved all of the modern conveniences. But he had to admit that his place lacked character. Sometimes it felt like he was living in a Williams Sonoma catalog. Winnie claimed it needed a woman's touch.

Lola plopped down in his oversize chair and pushed her long hair over her shoulder. All of a sudden, his condo started feeling a lot homier.

"Okay, time for operation get to know each other," she said with a nod.

"Well, not yet."

He jogged into the kitchen and returned with two bottles of beer. "You like? Wait, you're probably into wine, aren't you?"

"First lesson on Lola McBride," she said with a smile. "I prefer beer to wine."

"You're full of surprises." He opened both bottles of beer

with his trusty bottle opener shaped like the Golden Gate bridge and handed one over to her. "Have you eaten yet?"

She shook her head.

"Let me order us some dinner. I know you like pizza, but since you just had that, do you want burgers, Chinese, or something else?"

"Oooh, a burger sounds great."

He pulled up his UberEATS app and ordered two burgers from a nearby place, an order of fries for Lola and onion rings for himself. Then, they settled back in to get to know each other.

"I'm not sure where to start," Luke said.

"You already know I like beer and burgers. Let's see…" She tapped her finger against her lips, drawing his attention there like a moth to a flame. "My favorite color's pink. I like to go to the movies."

"What's your favorite movie?"

"*The Notebook*."

Luke couldn't help it. His eyes rolled of their own accord. "Of course it is."

"What's that supposed to mean?"

He gestured at her with his beer. "Can you explain to me why every woman in the world loves that movie? It's so depressing."

She let out a strangled sound. "What the hell is wrong with you? Number one"—she began ticking off her fingers—"Ryan Gosling. Number two, it's a beautiful love story. Number three, Ryan Gosling."

"I think I'm seeing a pattern here."

"What's your favorite movie?"

"I dunno. *Star Wars* probably. Or maybe *Goonies*."

She smiled. "Good choices."

"Even though Ryan Gosling isn't in them?"

She wiggled her eyebrows. "Young Harrison Ford and

young Josh Brolin are."

"Women." He threw his hands in the air and made her laugh.

An hour later, their burgers had been delivered and consumed. Luke handed Lola another beer and settled back into his comfy couch with his own. They'd been talking nonstop, and he had to admit that he enjoyed getting to know her.

She wasn't like other women he'd dated. The night they met he'd thought she seemed more genuine than most people. Tonight only confirmed that notion. She was real and sincere. Nothing phony about her. She answered every question he came up with, giving thought to each answer.

He glanced at her now. She took a sip of beer and then wiped her mouth with her napkin, before throwing it on her empty plate.

"That burger was great."

She grinned, which lit up her eyes. Luke could tell, even with her glasses on. It was like a fist to the gut. He was so drawn to her smile.

Sitting back against the cushion of the chair, she got comfortable. "So, we've covered favorite colors, movies, bands, and foods. Plus, we talked about past vacations and future wish-list destinations."

"We also know first concerts and first kisses." He snickered.

"Stop making fun of me." She threw the cap of her beer at him, which Luke easily caught. "I swear I had no idea."

"What did the guy say to you again?"

She turned her head and kept her lips firmly shut.

"Oh yes. He said that he loved French things and wanted to show you something from France." Luke burst out laughing. "That is the cheesiest line ever, and trust me I've used some bad ones."

She joined him on the couch and shoved his shoulder.

"Shut up. I was young and impressionable."

"But you had to see right through his motives for getting you alone."

She guffawed. "Hardly. He said he needed a French tutor, and I was really good in French class."

"Apparently your tongue was quite good, too." He winked at her, and she hit him again.

"Anyway…we need to come up with some stories about our relationship now," she said.

"What do you mean?"

"Surely your family is going to ask how we met. That's always the first question when you start dating someone new."

Good point. He hadn't thought of that but should have. With his busybody mom and aunts, not to mention his overly curious sisters, they were sure to grill him on Lola.

"Why don't we tell the truth? It will be easier on us to not have to remember a lie."

She pinned him with a stare. Even though looks were silent, this one screamed are-you-freaking-kidding-me.

"What?" he asked on a laugh. He couldn't help but be amused by her.

"Fake relationship or not, there is no way I'm going to tell your family that I met you by dressing all crazy and sneaking into a reunion that I was not invited to."

He remembered how Lola looked the night they met. He'd thought she was the most beautiful woman he'd seen in a long, long time. "I don't think you looked crazy that night."

She jabbed a finger into his chest. "That's what you get out of my statement. Do you really think I go around dressed like that?"

You should. Luke grinned. "Nothing wrong with a short dress. It was flattering."

"It was indecent."

"Not from where I was standing."

"Men." She shook her head. "Don't make me spill Jell-O on you again."

Luke raised his hands in surrender. "Okay, okay. You're bringing out the big guns. Still, I think my mom would get a kick out of our story."

Our story. Luke froze at his own words. They sounded so intimate. When was the last time he shared a story with a woman?

"There is no way on earth I'm going to tell your mother about that. 'Hi, Mrs. Erickson, so nice to meet you. I crashed an event in a ridiculous outfit, spilled Jell-O on your son, and stole a prize basket from an actual alum when I first met Luke.'" She blew out a breath, which caused her bangs to flutter.

"Okay, fine. If we can't go with the truth, what do you want to say?"

She twirled her beer bottle in her hand as she considered. "Why don't we say we met online? Isn't that how most people meet now?"

He supposed it was. He had a ton of friends who met on Tinder and Bumble. Still, he'd never actually signed up for any online dating sites or apps. One of his sisters—probably Gwen—was sure to call him out on it. But since Lola didn't want to tell the truth, he'd go with it.

"Fine. We met online. Not that exciting, but hopefully it will suffice."

Lola was staring at the door to his balcony. A dreamy expression crossed her face. The setting sun was streaming into his condo. She was aglow with the light from the sunset.

"That's beautiful."

So was she.

Luke shook his head. He had to stop. He couldn't keep having thoughts like this about Lola. Not while they were pretending to be dating for his family's sake.

Still, he couldn't take his eyes off her. When was the last

time he'd felt such a strong physical pull toward a woman?

"Come on," he said suddenly. He rose and crossed to the balcony door, sliding it open and waiting for her to join him. "I have to admit that the view and the balcony sold me on buying this place."

He led her outside where he had a small table and two chairs. In one corner, his grill sat, cover on. At the other end of the space was a small herb garden. Flowers bloomed from boxes hanging over the ledge. All of the plants were a contribution from his sisters. Winnie often stopped by to make sure he was watering them.

Lola sat in one chair, and he took the other. Their beers were on the table. A mixture of smells wafted up to them from the restaurants below. Between the Indian place, the all-American pub, and the Thai restaurant, his nose was assaulted with a bevy of aromas.

They sat in comfortable silence, observing the changing sky. A large red orb held court in the middle of orange, pink, and yellow streaks across the sky. It made for a gorgeous end of day and beginning of night.

"I would spend all my time out here," Lola finally said.

"It's great." Unfortunately, he didn't use this space as much as he should.

"Do you barbeque often?" she asked, gesturing toward the grill.

"Sometimes." Again, not as often as he should. "I haven't lived here all that long yet, though."

"I can't believe you own a place. That's wild. It's so expensive around here."

"True, but not as expensive as Manhattan."

She nodded, as if accepting the validity of his statement. "Which neighborhood did you live in there?"

"A couple. But most of my time was spent in Tribeca."

"I like that area," she said. "Are you happy you moved

back here?"

Luke had mixed feelings. He liked the D.C.-area. But there were demons here he wished would hide. Unfortunately, he'd found that running away hadn't helped.

He didn't want to get into all that with Lola though. "It's been pretty uneventful. Well, until last Saturday when I met this person who's subjected me to reunion crashing and runaway dogs."

She laughed and took a sip of beer. "Should we go over more personal questions?"

He choked on his beer. "More? How could you have more? I think you know everything about me. More than my best friend. All my deep, dark secrets."

"Hm." She tilted her head. "What size shoe do you wear?"

Luke was torn between rolling his eyes and letting out a chuckle. Lola was nothing if not thorough. "Do you really think my family is going to care—or even wonder at all—if we know each other's shoe sizes?"

She nailed him with a solemn stare.

"Okay, fine." He gave in to the eye roll. "I wear a thirteen."

She did something he didn't expect. Her eyes widened and immediately flicked down to his lap.

What?

Then it hit him. The old adage of big feet, big…other parts. His face felt hot. Holy hell, was he blushing now? He snuck a glance at Lola. Her eyes were still clamped on his lap, and her cheeks were redder than the setting sun.

"Sorry, I didn't mean to ask that."

"Uh, that's okay. No big deal," he said.

"Great. Cuz, you know what they say?" She groaned.

"Yeah, I know. And I do."

"Do what?" Her eyes flipped up to meet his.

"Have big feet. And, you know…"

"Oh. Oh! Um…well, great. That's good to know."

He scrubbed a hand over his face. "I'm not trying to brag, but I just mean, well, if we're dating, we've surely…" He moved his hand back and forth between them.

"Right," she said quickly. "We would definitely have done *that*."

"So you would know about my, uh…"

"Shoe size," she finished for him. If it was possible, the color on her face grew even brighter.

Luke took a long—very, very long—swig of his beer. The cold liquid did nothing to extinguish his boiling libido. Suddenly he felt incredibly uncomfortable, especially in the pants area.

Great. Now all he was thinking about was his big feet. And sex. Sex with Lola. Sex on the balcony. Sex on the balcony with Lola, his big feet planted firmly on the concrete as he took her from behind.

Stop it.

Was Lola feeling this shift in the atmosphere? Was she thinking about having sex on the balcony? Lola wasn't looking at him. Her gaze seemed to be cloudy as she ran a hand down the column of her neck. She was sitting next to him, her long legs crossed over each other and her ample chest rising and falling with every breath she took.

Then there were those lips. Those enticing, succulent lips. If he closed his eyes he could remember how they felt against his. Hell, he didn't even need to close his eyes. He could recall their kiss perfectly. Every nip, every tease.

And he wanted to do it again. And again and again.

Get it together.

He pointed to her nearly empty beer bottle. "Do you want another kiss?"

Lola coughed. "What?"

"Beer," he shouted. "Do you want another beer?"

"We kissed yesterday," she blurted out.

He froze. "We did." This was it. The moment he really didn't want to have. A conversation about their kiss. He'd much rather go back to his daydreaming and forget all about reality, because once they talked about what happened between them, it would be out there. Real.

His daydreams could stay firmly in his mind.

Luke cleared his throat. "The thing is…"

"You didn't like it." She bit her lip.

"What? No. I mean, yes. I mean, yes, I liked it. A lot. A whole lot."

"Really?"

"Really." His gaze clamped down on those lips now. Honing in on them served as a potent reminder.

Her lips twitched before blossoming into a sweet smile. That smile served as a reminder that Lola was a good girl. She was kind and charming. Totally not the kind of girl he usually went out with a couple of times before breaking things off. The truth of the matter was that she was only acting as his pretend girlfriend. After his family reunion this weekend, it would be over.

He didn't want to hurt her, but he knew he was going to. Flicking a finger between them, he said, "What we're doing here is pretend. It's not real."

"I know that."

"It's just that I don't want to lead you on."

Instantly, her smile faded. "Then why did you kiss me yesterday?"

"Because you were sad."

Her brows drew together. "No, I wasn't."

"You were telling me about your parents."

She shook her head. "My parents died. It's sad, but I'm used to it. It's my life. I wasn't feeling particular down that afternoon."

He remembered her face. If that wasn't sadness, he didn't

know what was. How could she not be sad every time she talked about her parents?

She pushed her chair back. It made a scraping sound against the concrete floor of the balcony. The abrupt sound had his head snapping up.

"I don't want you to feel bad for me," she said. "And I definitely don't want you, or anyone else, to pity kiss me."

"I didn't—"

"And another thing. I can find my own people to kiss. There are tons of guys…"

"I thought you just went through a breakup."

She harrumphed. "I did." She blew a breath and made her bangs flutter. "It's not like I'm some sad Sally who sits around pining all day to be kissed."

He stood as well. "Of course you're not. You're beautiful and smart and—"

"Oh please. Do me a favor and don't finish that sentence. I know exactly who I am." She crossed to the balcony door. Her hand hovered over the handle, shaking slightly. "You shouldn't have kissed me."

He definitely shouldn't have kissed her. But he had. Now he had to fix the situation. "Lola, I told you I don't do relationships. At least, not real ones. I don't want to hurt you."

Her face fell. All the air left his lungs, and the same sadness he saw there yesterday returned. It had never been his intention to make her feel bad.

"Let me make it easy on you then. I'll leave so you don't have another opportunity to hurt me."

With that, she opened the door, slid through it, closed it quickly, and fled his condo. Stunned, Luke remained outside.

He'd broken up with dozens of girls over the years, but somehow breaking up with his pretend girlfriend left him with some very real pain.

Chapter Six

"I could vomit just looking at you."
-Dorothy Zbornak

"He said what?"

Lola sighed at Frankie's question. She really didn't want to talk about Luke Erickson anymore. But since Frankie had been asleep when she'd returned the night before, this was their first opportunity to dish in person. Naturally, they'd been texting about the situation all day long.

"No way did he say he kissed you because you were sad," Frankie continued before Lola could answer her first question. "I mean, were you sad?"

"No. I don't know. Maybe a little bit. I was telling him about my parents." She shrugged. "But if Luke went around kissing every woman who looked sad then he'd, well, he'd…"

"Have some really chapped lips," Frankie finished for her. "Besides the horrible ending, how was the rest of the night?"

Lola flopped down onto the couch, a large sigh following

in her wake. "It was great. Really fun actually."

"That's a shame." Frankie joined her. "So what's going to happen with his family reunion this weekend?"

Lola repressed a groan that wanted to escape. She really, really didn't want to think about his family reunion. On the one hand, she'd made him a promise, and she didn't like reneging on promises. But on the other, well, there was no way in hell she was going now.

To answer Frankie's question she threw her hands over her face, leaned back on the couch, and finally let out that groan. "I'm doing what I always do."

"What would that be?"

Lola removed her hands from her face and sat up straight. She pointed an accusatory finger at Frankie. "You know."

Frankie stuck her nose in the air. "I know nothing."

"Yes, you do. You're my best friend, and sometimes you know me better than I know myself. Therefore, you are perfectly aware that I always do this. I don't say what I mean in the moment. I say something, but it doesn't make me feel better. Then, here I am, almost an entire day later and I'm beating myself up for not having stood up for myself." Exhausted, she collapsed against the cushions of the couch.

"Sadly, it's true. You don't stick up for yourself. Why? I'm not sure. You have everything in the world going for you."

"I wish I could see what you see when you look at me."

Frankie's face softened. "So do I. And anyway, there's a simple solution to this problem. You need to find your voice." Frankie paused, her face deep in thought. "Find your voice and then use it."

Her best friend's words warmed her heart. "Aw, thanks, Frankie."

"Well, I mean it. I wish you would have stuck up for yourself with Mark when he broke up with you."

Lola hugged a pillow close to her chest. "Oh God, me

too. See, that's another time. I stood there and let him tell me that he was leaving me to date someone younger."

"Don't forget prettier, too."

"Thanks, Frankie."

"Shut up. I don't think she was prettier than you. I'm simply repeating what douchey-doucherson said. You know what you should have said back to him?"

This time, Lola didn't need to think about it. She'd already been doing that for the last couple weeks. "I should have told him that he was a classless jerkwad for saying something so hurtful to someone else. I should have pointed out that he's not God's gift. He has flaws. Like his nose hair."

"His nose hair? Ew." Frankie laughed, even as she cringed.

"When you got up close to him, it was sooo obvious. Boy needed to go in for a trim. Like yesterday. And he belched under his breath all the time. As if I couldn't hear it. Covering your mouth with your hand when you burp does not render the other person deaf all of a sudden."

Frankie started bouncing on the couch. "What else? What else?"

"He wasn't that good of a kisser. I mean, was that his tongue or a plunger?"

"Yuck! Anything else?"

Lola straightened her shoulders. "Yes. I should have told him that I was too good for him. That he was lucky to have dated me. And that he could…well, he could…"

"Come on, Lo. You can say it," Frankie said.

"He could go fuck himself."

Frankie punched her arm into the air. "Yes! That's my girl. How do you feel?"

She took a deep breath and counted to five. Lola waited for the onslaught of guilt to filter through her. She didn't normally say negative things about people. Of course, that was probably why people usually walked all over her.

At the moment, she actually felt kind of good. Alive. "I feel both exhausted and empowered."

"Great. Now let's tell Luke Erickson to fuck off, too."

Just like that her mood plummeted at the mention of Luke. She wanted to say something to him, but it wasn't *that*.

"Oh, Lola, what's with the sad face?" Frankie moved closer and draped an arm around her shoulders.

"I don't know. I guess I...I don't know."

"Hm, maybe you really liked that kiss with Luke and wanted it to be real. When he told you he only kissed you because he thought you were sad, it hurt you."

Bingo. Even though Luke had already told her that he didn't do relationships, she'd still believed that he'd meant that kiss. How could something that had felt so amazing not been real?

"Do you like him, Lo?"

"Does it matter? He doesn't believe in relationships."

Frankie watched her for a long moment. "That's not an answer." She glanced out the window behind the couch. "Let me ask you this. What would you do if you saw him right here, right now?"

"I don't know. Why?"

"Because he's headed up the front steps." She pointed toward the window.

Lola jumped up and looked outside, but she didn't see anything. Which meant Luke was already in the building.

"Ohmigod, ohmigod. What am I gonna do? I don't want to see him right now."

"Calm down," Frankie said at the same time a knock sounded at the door. "I'll deal with this. You stay here."

"Thanks, Frankie."

Lola watched as Frankie crossed to the door. She cracked it open and spoke in hushed tones, except for when she uttered, "You've gotta be kidding me. You're good." Shaking her head, she closed the door gently, turned, and walked back to the living room.

"Is he gone?"

"Um, no."

"What do you mean no? You were supposed to get rid of him."

Frankie threw her hands up. "He really wants to talk to you."

"Well, I don't want to talk to him."

"He wants to apologize and trust me when I say this, he's come armed and dangerous."

"What does that mean?"

"Go see for yourself."

Frustrated, but also curious, Lola slowly and begrudgingly shuffled to the door. She glanced back at Frankie, who simply smiled and nodded. She took a deep breath, which did nothing to calm her, and yanked open the door.

She was about to channel her inner confidence when a definitive bark sounded. Startled, she stepped back and looked down.

"A dog? You have a dog?"

Luke shot her a devastatingly hot grin. He managed to be both boyish and sexy in one gesture. Her pulse picked up.

"Hey," he said.

"*Arf.*"

"Um, hi?" She couldn't help but ruffle the fur on the dog's head. He was an adorable black and white mix. He looked like a baby panda. Lola crouched down so they were eye level. "Aren't you cute."

"Why thank you. Oh, you meant the dog." Luke joined her. "This is Ralphie. He's a friend's dog. I'm watching him for the night while my friend is out of town at a business meeting."

Lola continued to pet Ralphie, who was eating up the attention. His tongue hung out of his mouth, and his tail was wagging a hundred miles a minute. Unable to resist, Lola began lavishing even more attention on him and using her best doggie-baby-voice.

"Aren't you sweet? You're just the cutest little boy ever. Yes, you are. You're so handsome. The handsomest boy ever."

When she'd gotten her fill, she sat back on her heels and glanced up at Luke. "So why'd you bring Ralphie here?"

"I wanted to talk to you, but I assumed you might not want to talk to me."

"You assumed correctly."

Ralphie flipped onto his back, and Luke obediently crouched and rubbed his tummy. The dog's excited legs went wild.

"I'd like to apologize to you." His gaze flicked up to meet hers. "And to explain."

"You could have texted."

"You could have ignored that."

He had her there. Seemed Luke Erickson thought of everything.

"I figured there was no way you could say no to this adorable dog. I mean, look at his big brown eyes and hopeful expression."

She was too busy looking at Luke's big brown eyes and hopeful expression. She felt her willpower dissipating, not to mention, she *was* curious.

"I don't know…"

"Just come for a walk with me. With Ralphie. He's dying to get outside."

Ralphie was currently busy licking his privates. Lola didn't claim to be a pet whisperer, but if she had to guess, Ralphie was probably quite content.

Frankie coughed in the background. Lola peeked over

her shoulder, and Frankie made a shooing gesture with her hands.

"Fine," she finally said to Luke. "Let's go for a walk."

At the word *walk* Ralphie leaped up, his tail showing his excitement. He practically bounced down the hallway.

Lola grabbed her flip-flops, and they exited the building into the warm evening air. The sun hadn't quite set yet, and plenty of people were milling about the street. Even when the light was completely gone, the Shirlington neighborhood would remain active. Tables were placed outside every restaurant and bar. Twinkly lights were strung on the trees that lined the street with the cobblestone sidewalks.

They walked in silence for a while. Lola was enjoying Ralphie. She'd even taken over leash duty. Not shy in the slightest, Ralphie pranced down the sidewalk, greeting giggling children and going up to people dining outdoors.

For a special treat, they took him into the neighborhood dog store where he filled up on free treats from the doggy bakery. He met a French Bulldog and seemed to have fun playing.

They continued their stroll around the neighborhood, Ralphie leading the way. He'd stop to lap up water from the bowls that the local establishments provided for all the dogs.

It all felt so normal. Like they were a real couple who did this every night after dinner. Only they weren't a real couple. And she hadn't even eaten dinner that night.

Lola dreamed of a time when she would have someone to come home to. They would talk about their days as they ate a healthy and well-rounded meal that she somehow miraculously learned to cook. They would go on romantic weekend getaways. Maybe they would get a dog.

Lola let out a long sigh at that thought.

"What is it?" Luke asked.

"Nothing."

"Want to talk about last night?"

"Not really," she said.

While she really didn't want to talk about their fight, Lola was impressed that Luke had come over at all. In the grand scheme of things, he didn't need to. She wasn't anything to him. He could have ghosted, as if she'd never entered his life.

"I'd like to," he said. "I want to apologize, Lola."

She bit her lip. It took a lot to admit you were wrong. She had to hand that to Luke. "So you didn't mean what you said? You didn't kiss me because you thought I was sad?"

Luke stopped at a bench. He sat down, and Ralphie made himself comfortable under the bench, content to rest and people watch. Lola joined him.

"I did think you were sad the other day when we had lunch, and that's why I kissed you."

"Oh."

"But it wasn't the only reason," he added.

Lola felt her eyebrow rise in surprise. "It wasn't?"

He shook his head. "I'm attracted to you. I know you probably hear this all the time, but you're kinda gorgeous."

Her mouth fell open. "Huh?"

"Don't act like you've never heard that before," he said with a laugh.

"My last boyfriend broke up with me because I wasn't pretty enough. He found someone younger and more beautiful than me."

"Sounds like a real prince."

"He was special."

Luke swiveled toward her, stretching his arm over the back of the bench. "That guy sucks, but I don't. At least, I don't want you to think I do."

"I still don't get why you kissed me."

"It's simple. I like you, Lola."

. . .

Admitting he liked her wasn't as hard as he thought. The truth was Luke did like Lola, a lot.

He snuck a glance at her now and saw the confusion on her face. Understandable.

A crease formed on her forehead. "But you don't like relationships," she said.

"I don't believe in them."

"What does that mean exactly?" She twisted her long hair into a knot and then let it fall around her face again. "Have you never been in a romantic relationship? Will you go your entire life without being in one? What about when you're sixty? Will you be content to live all alone? And then what happens if you get sick, and who will be your beneficiary for your 401k and—"

"Whoa, whoa, whoa. Back up a few decades." Luke laughed and held his hands up.

She relented with a half smile. "Sorry."

Luke took a deep breath. He didn't particularly enjoy talking about what he was about to reveal. In fact, it was rare that he would bring it up at all. But Lola was different. It was so much more than her physical appearance. When they had a conversation, he felt like he was the only person in the city. She listened to him, really listened. Because of that, he felt like he could be himself with her.

"My dad left us when I was little."

Her eyes widened. "Oh, I'm sorry."

"Thanks. It was a long time ago though." That was his standard comeback. So when he kept going, he surprised himself. "But it still hurts as much today as it did back then."

"Does it feel like something's missing in your life?"

Exactly. He nodded. "I was five and my sisters were four. It was really tough."

Ralphie let out a tiny bark, like he understood. Luke reached down to pet him for a few moments.

"It wasn't just that he left. A lot of people's parents get divorced. It was the way he did it and the way he was afterward."

"What do you mean?"

"One day he got up and announced he was leaving. That was it. Like he was deciding he no longer liked a certain TV show. Done with that. Next. My sister Winnie used to say she felt like a shoe."

"A shoe?"

"Like my dad bought a pair of shoes and when he got home he decided he didn't actually want them anymore."

"Wow, that's really harsh," Lola said. "He never gave you any reasons why he abandoned you?"

Hearing the word *abandon* always felt like someone punched him in the gut. You abandoned bags of garbage, not a wife and kids. He wasn't something for someone to dispose of. Although, that's exactly what had happened.

"One time, not too long after he left, he said that he wasn't dad material. The life he was living wasn't for him."

Lola's mouth dropped. "He said that to a five-year-old?"

"I think I was six by that time, but yeah. Probably thought I didn't understand and wouldn't remember. But I did, on both counts."

"Do you have any contact with him now?"

"None. The first couple years he tried." He used air-quotes when he said the word *tried*. "Cards, presents, phone calls, that sort of thing. Even as a child, I didn't buy it. Neither did my sisters. Gwen especially. She'd also been the closest with him. Something about his efforts just never felt genuine."

"Kids are intuitive, more so than adults usually," Lola said.

"When I started dating, I guess I realized how fragile

relationships really were. A person can up and peace out like that." He snapped his fingers together. "If a certificate of marriage isn't enough to keep a person grounded, what's supposed to keep a couple with no legal ties together?"

Feeling worked up, he took a moment to collect himself. "To answer one of your earlier questions, I have been in relationships. None of them worked out."

"So why even try," she said.

"Exactly."

She grabbed his shoulders, forcing him to look right in her eyes. "No, Luke. You still have to try. I'm not saying that you need to be in a relationship with me, but at some point in your life you have to be brave enough to let another person inside." She rapped a knuckle against his chest.

"Why?" He croaked out the question, his voice scratchy and his eyes burning.

"Because you're missing out on so much. Think of the possibilities."

Luke grimaced. "Think of what my dad did to my mom. Think of how hurt she must have been."

Lola scooted closer to him on the bench. "I'm thinking about how hurt you must have been. How hurt you still are."

She was right, and all that hurt was currently balled up in his throat, making it difficult to speak.

"You stay out of relationships because you're afraid the other person will leave. You don't want to get hurt."

That wasn't right. He shook his head, willing his throat to clear so he could explain properly.

"No. I don't want to be like my father. I don't get into relationships because I don't ever want to cause another person that level of pain."

Lola placed a soft hand against his cheek. "You're not worried about yourself?"

He covered her hand with his. "I'm worried about the

other person. What if I'm like my dad? What if I also decide that the life I'm living isn't exactly for me?"

He realized he was admitting more to her tonight than he had in a long time. Maybe ever. Even to himself.

"Sometimes, even all these years later, I obsess about my dad leaving us. Over twenty years later, and the pain is just as real, just as raw. I guess when you told me about your mom and dad the other day, I thought I knew how you felt. My dad left me, and your parents left you. I know they're not comparable situations."

"Aw, I think I get it now."

"But maybe you're better at handling your pain that I am."

She looked thoughtful. "I think people handle their issues in different ways. Besides, it's not the same situation. My parents are gone and nothing can bring them back. But you, well, your dad is still around. Somewhere. In a way, that's probably even harder."

Exactly. No one had ever honed in on it so accurately before. Not his mom, not his sisters, not the counselor he'd seen in elementary school. His dad was out there, somewhere, living his life. Did he ever wonder about his son, his daughters, his ex-wife?

"So you understand why I'm not into relationships. They turn sour."

At this point—if Luke even let things get this far—most girls had heard enough. The ones who enjoyed a challenge would persist. Try to break him down. Challenge accepted. Others would roll their eyes, storm out, stop following him on Instagram and Snapchat. The Millennial cold shoulder.

But Lola looked…thoughtful, he decided. She adjusted her glasses.

"I don't know," she said.

"What?"

"Your whole theory isn't very substantiated. Take my parents, for example. They were married for twenty years. Well, before my dad passed away."

"Do you think they'd be together today if they were alive?"

"Yes," she said without hesitation. "Their relationship was beautiful, their stories wonderful."

He looked down at his feet, kicking at an imaginary stone with one of them.

"Don't get me wrong," Lola continued and touched his forearm. "Things weren't perfect. Every day wasn't a second honeymoon. They fought. They drove each other crazy. My dad would walk around the house and floss his teeth, and my mom hated that. My mom wasn't a good cleaner, and my dad was OCD. But that's what was great. Their relationship was real."

Her eyes lit up as she spoke about her parents. In fact, they practically sparkled as a huge smile blossomed on her face.

"What are you thinking about now?" he asked.

"Hm? Oh. I was thinking about one of my favorite stories. My parents' first date."

She sat back, a dreamy expression on her face. It was as if she was instantly transported to another time, another place.

"I thought it was at the movie theater."

She shook her head. "Nope. That was where they met. Their official first date was the next night."

"My mom was Italian so my dad took her to an Italian restaurant in Georgetown."

"Ciao Bella?" It was a popular place on the corner of M Street and Wisconsin. Tourists loved it.

She scrunched up her nose. "Nah. That place is a chain and way overpriced. He found this little hole in the wall called Ristorante Formaggi."

"Cheese Restaurant?" he said translating the name with a chuckle.

"My dad always said don't judge a restaurant by its name, a cheese by its smell, or a movie by its trailer."

Luke let her dad's words soak in. He bet he would have liked Mr. McBride. More than that, he was really starting to like his daughter.

Speaking of not judging a book by its cover, Lola McBride continued to surprise him.

"Anyway, Ristorante Formaggi is in this tiny building. Maybe an old row house they converted. It doesn't seat that many. The tables are wobbly, and they have candles out that look like they're a million years old. My mom said it was incredibly romantic. Like being in an old movie." Lola bit her lip. "They used to go back there every year for their anniversary."

"That's sweet."

"They even remembered what they got to eat. My dad had the eggplant parmesan and my mom had the gnocchi. She said it was almost as good as her mother's. Almost, but not quite."

"Now you're making me hungry," he said.

"So, after this amazing dinner of wonderful and authentic Italian food they went for a walk."

"Wait, wait, wait." Luke waved his hands. "I knew it was too good to be true."

"What are you talking about?"

"They didn't have dessert?"

She smiled. "Is that all you think of? Dessert?"

"Hell yes. And Italian places have some of the best. Tell me they got cannoli."

"Sorry, they went for the tiramisu."

"Everyone always does. But I'm telling you, splitting a cannoli is the way to go."

"Do you want to hear the rest of this story or not?"

"I don't know. I feel jaded now." He leaned back against the bench.

"How about I let you change that one little detail. My parents split a damn cannoli."

"That's all I ask. Proceed. After they split their cannoli, they went for a walk."

"Yes, they headed down by the Georgetown waterfront, along the Potomac River. They ended up at the Lincoln Memorial."

"Everyone should see the monuments at night," Luke said. They were a spectacular sight.

"Mom used to say that, too, but she always added that you should see them with someone you love."

"Was that the end of the date?"

"Actually, no. They ended up talking. All night. In fact, they also got to see the sunrise over the monuments. Another thing that everyone should do according to my dad."

Luke nodded. He'd tried to do that once at the end of his senior year of high school. He and a bunch of his friends woke at the buttcrack of dawn, trekked down to the monuments and set up camp to watch the sunrise. Unfortunately, it had been overcast that morning, and they'd never seen them.

Lola hit him lightly in the chest. "Can you imagine? A first date that is so amazing that you spend the entire night together."

Luke wiggled his eyebrows, and Lola smacked him again. "Not like that, perv. They talked and talked. Can you imagine having that kind of chemistry with another person?"

He turned to face her fully. He looked past those glasses at the light blue of her eyes. He watched the way she spoke so passionately that her cheeks flushed. Yes, he could imagine having chemistry like that with someone. He was sitting with that someone right now.

"They knew that early," Lola said. "They got that there was something special between them."

Luke's heart rate sped up. Hadn't he just admitted to himself that he'd told Lola more tonight than he'd ever told anyone?

Shit. He was falling hard for her.

"Can you even fathom what that's like?" she asked.

Luke honed in on her lips. Those perfect, pouty lips.

He didn't think. He didn't overanalyze. He just went for it.

Luke leaned toward her and pressed his mouth to hers. For one long moment, they stayed like that, lips pressed together on a bench in the middle of town. She shivered, and he pulled her closer, wrapping his arms around her tightly. Then he kissed the hell out of her.

It was like every good sensation he'd ever experienced in his life came together to form this one perfect kiss. They were so in sync. But, of course, they would be. Their conversations were flawless. They had a good time together. So naturally their mouths were made for each other, too.

When he pulled back with much reluctance, he took a moment to push some of her bangs to the side. Really, it was to give himself some time to get his roaring pulse back to normal.

"I kissed you," he said.

She let out a cute little sigh. "I noticed that." Her voice was breathy, and the sound of it filled him with pride that he was the cause.

"To be clear, the reason I did it was because…well…"

She waited patiently. Or so it seemed. When he glanced down she was clenching and unclenching her fingers nervously.

"I didn't kiss you because you were sad or angry or any other emotion. I kissed you because I couldn't *not* kiss you in that moment."

She let out a whoosh of breath. "Oh."

"Yeah. Oh."

"I'm not sure where this puts us," she said, a line forming on her forehead. "You don't do relationships and I, well, do. But we keep kissing."

He ran a hand over his head. "How about we not think too hard about it. Let's concentrate on my family reunion this weekend, and we'll worry about the kissing later."

Lola agreed. They walked back to her apartment, Ralphie in tow.

After he dropped her off with another stunner of a kiss goodnight, Luke took his time walking with the dog. He'd meant what he'd said to her. They should focus on his reunion this weekend. Because, honestly, if he let his mind think about her—really think about her—he would have to admit that he was in big trouble.

For the first time in forever, the word relationship didn't seem quite so scary.

Chapter Seven

"Like we say in St. Olaf – Christmas without fruitcake is like St. Sigmund's Day without the headless boy."
-Rose Nylund

"Lola McBride, you are the most gorgeous woman on the planet, and your outfit blows all other outfits out of the water."

Normally, she would have preened at the compliment, but at the moment, she chose to ignore Luke, who was impatiently yelling at her from the living room.

Men really didn't understand. This was the big day. She was meeting his family. Not any ordinary family, either. Luke had told her who would be in attendance. All women. His mom, her two sisters, Luke's triplet sisters, and a handful of cousins. Girl cousins.

What did she know about girls? That no matter how impressed they were with your conversation and wit, they would definitely dissect your outfit after you left.

"I thought you had picked something," Luke said. He sounded closer, like he was right outside her door. "Didn't you text me last night that Frankie helped you narrow down the options?"

"Yes," she shouted back. "She helped me narrow it down to three choices." She wrenched the door open to find Luke with one arm extended up above him to the top of the doorframe and the other roaming over his face.

"Everything you've shown me looks amazing. Besides, we're going to a picnic in a park, not to visit the Queen of England."

"Speaking of the picnic, are you sure what I'm bringing is okay?" She'd picked up a huge platter of fruit that morning.

"What? Oh yeah. Whatever. You didn't need to bring anything."

She pinned him with a stare. "This is the first time I'm meeting your mother. Of course I have to bring something. I was going to bake some cookies. I make pretty decent chocolate chip." She began toying with different earrings, holding them up to her ears and checking it out in the mirror. "But you said your sister worked in a bakery. No way I can compete with that."

Seemingly at home, Luke flopped down on her bed. "Do you worry about everything?"

"Yes," she answered easily. "Guys never understand. It's the little things that truly matter. Speaking of, maybe I should go with the other tank top." She gnawed on her lip and then silently chastised herself because she'd just applied her lipstick.

He shot up. "No, don't do it. You look amazing. Better than amazing. Phenomenal." His brows drew together as he thought. "Spectacular."

"Oh please." She turned to her closet, which now didn't hold much thanks to the piles of discarded options strewn throughout her room. She placed a finger to her lips as she considered. "I know."

"Lolaaaaa," Luke said.

"No, just give me one minute. You can stay on my bed. I'll run to the bathroom and slip this on."

Okay, so it was more like five minutes than one, but Lola thought those three hundred seconds were totally worth it. The short leggings and long tank top with a glittery flower on it were perfect. Cool enough for an outdoor picnic. It was cute and fun without being too revealing.

She burst back into her room. Luke was holding a picture frame. He glanced up and a grin lit up his face.

"Hey, you look great."

She did a little spin. "Not amazing, phenomenal, or spectacular," she said teasingly.

He crossed to her. Cupping her cheek, he pulled her face to his and planted a soft kiss on her lips. It was such a boyfriend-y thing to do. Lola had to work hard to keep the sigh in.

When he moved to end the kiss, she indulged by deepening the connection. She opened her mouth and welcomed his eager tongue. Their arms twined around each other as they moved even closer. He smelled so good. Like soap from his morning shower and a fresh, earthy scent from his cologne. She could just eat him up, which might happen if she let the kiss go on any longer. Regretfully, she pulled back.

"You must really like this outfit," she said lightly, even though she was actually feeling quite serious. Good thing he was holding her, because her knees were about to buckle.

"You should see what I do if you pick the right shoes."

She laughed as she threw some of her clothes back into her closet. She hated leaving a messy room behind.

"Hey, Lola," he said softly.

She turned back to him. His face was serious.

"Thanks for doing this. It, uh, really means a lot to me."

She nodded. "You're welcome."

After another couple minutes of grabbing everything she would need, including switching purses, they were ready to go. Off to meet the family of her pretend boyfriend.

· · ·

Lola thought she was going to be sick. She had enough nerves dancing around her stomach that they could fuel the car.

She tried to remind herself that this wasn't real. If Mrs. Erickson didn't like her or one of Luke's sisters thought she was lame, it didn't matter in the grand scheme of things. They weren't dating.

She was merely helping him out. Getting his family off his back for a little while.

"Lola," Luke said, as he threw his car into park when they arrived.

"Yeah?"

"Breathe." He squeezed her hand. Then he unlocked her seatbelt for her, stopping for a chaste kiss.

They exited the car and walked a short way toward the pavilion the family had rented for the day. Lola could hear them long before she saw them. A bevy of raised female voices competing with each other for main voice carried to the pathway where they were walking.

She heard orders being barked out and demands for different things. She also heard a good deal of laughter.

"Sounds like we're the last ones to arrive," Luke said.

Damn. She should have just gone with her first outfit choice and then they would have been there earlier. She hated walking into a party when it was already in full swing.

But that's exactly what happened.

The path curved, and they walked out into a clearing with a wooden pavilion housing about half a dozen picnic tables and benches. There was a grill to the side of it on its own slab of concrete. Off to the left a few yards were swing sets and other toys for kids. The whole area was surrounded by verdant green grass and tall trees.

"Ready for this?" Luke whispered.

Nope, not at all. "Sure am," she responded with way more confidence than she felt.

"Luke," someone yelled out.

Lola wasn't sure who had said it, but it didn't matter. As soon as they did, every head under the pavilion swiveled in their direction. All conversation ceased, and no one moved.

Lola stepped closer to Luke, but Luke simply grinned and waved. "Hey, everyone. Come on," he said to Lola.

They walked closer. Lola noticed no one had moved yet. They were all too busy taking her in without any hints of subtlety. She gulped.

"Everyone, this is Lola. Lola, this is my family. Lola is my…girlfriend."

As soon as Luke finished, three women all said simultaneously in a sing-song rhythm, "Hi, Lola." She peered closer. They must be Luke's sisters. They wore identical smiles of mischief that perfectly matched a smile she'd seen on their brother.

A woman walked over to them with open arms. She was gorgeous. Her hair was a dark honey blond and cut into a stylish bob. Her skin was flawless, with only a few lines that spoke of age and experience. And her smile was kind and welcoming.

Lola liked her instantly.

Before she could say anything, the woman enveloped her in a tight and comforting hug. When she was done, she leaned back and took in Lola. "Welcome, sweetheart. We're so happy you're joining us today. For better or worse, I'm Luke's mother." She winked at her son.

"Thank you for having me, Mrs. Erickson."

She waved a hand. "Please, call me Lorraine."

Lola could see where Luke got his brown eyes from. They were exactly the same as his mother's. As the three girls moved forward, she noticed they had the same eyes as well.

"Lola, these three losers are my sisters. This is Winnie, Mia, and Gwen," he said gesturing from left to right.

Lola quickly tried to catalog each of them. They had the same general look and build, but each of them held their own unique qualities. All three of them were tall with legs for miles and killer curves. But Winnie had light red hair cut in a chic lob with a long sweep of side bangs. Mia's hair was long, golden blond, and held just a twinge of curl. Then there was Gwen, who was standing a step behind her two sisters giving Lola an assessing once-over. The color of her shoulder-length hair was a combination of her two sisters but ended in bright blue tips. It was cute, fun, and flirty. But somehow Lola got the idea that Gwen would not appreciate that description.

"Hi," Lola said.

Mia punched Luke in the arm. "Did you just call us losers?"

"I believe he did, Mimi. What do you think, Gwennie?"

Gwen finally inched closer, her fierce expression never fading. "I think we're going to kick his ass later when the water guns come out from hiding."

"Language, Gwen," Lorraine said. Luke stifled a laugh.

"Not those blasted water guns again. Every time they're together, someone has to be soaking wet."

"Or it's not a real party," Mia finished. "Lola, this is our Aunt Sally."

"Nice to meet you. Should I be afraid of these water guns?"

Winnie said no at the same time that Gwen said yes with an evil-looking grin.

"What did you bring us, Luke?" Mia asked.

Luke put the large tray on one of the picnic tables. "This is from Lola, actually. I brought my usual."

"Booze?" Gwen asked. Luke nodded. "Any scotch?" Luke nodded again. "Okay, then maybe I won't go too hard on you with the water gun."

For the first time, Lola saw a softening in Gwen's face. She hip-bumped her brother, and he pulled on the end of one of her blue-tipped locks. Maybe there was a marshmallow under all that bravado.

"What did Lola bring us then?" Winnie asked, uncovering the tray.

"She brought a fruit platter. Wasn't that nice?" Luke said, snagging a chip from a basket that had already been set out.

"Very nice. Thank you, Lola," Lorraine said.

Gwen scrunched her nose. "Fruit?"

"Gwen," Winnie said. "That was thoughtful, Lola."

"Fruit?" Gwen repeated.

Lola sighed. She'd had a feeling fruit wouldn't be that popular. She turned to Luke. "See, I knew they wouldn't like it."

Denials to her statement quickly poured out of everyone's mouths. Luke looked distraught, but Lola simply laughed and reached into her purse.

She whipped out two jars. "Chocolate," she said, holding one up. "And caramel," she finished by showing the other dip. "What goes better with fruit than chocolate and caramel?"

Gwen sauntered over to her and draped an arm around Lola's shoulders. "Our kind of woman."

. . .

Lola was having fun. She'd met a lot of people. A lot. Luke had a ton of cousins ranging in age from thirteen all the way up to his sisters' age of twenty-seven. All female and none married. He was the oldest of all these girls. Must have been interesting growing up.

She could also see why they all got on him about finding a wife and settling down. He was the only guy.

After she'd been introduced to Luke's mother and sisters, the rest of the family gathered around her. Luke wasn't kidding when he said he didn't do relationships and never brought dates to meet the family. She got the distinct impression she was something of a novelty. She was peppered with a barrage of rapid-fire questions.

Where are you from?
Where did you go to school?
Where do you live now?
What do you do?
Are you on Instagram?

That last question came from Michelle, Luke's youngest cousin. Lola took a deep breath and tried to answer every question. "I'm from Alexandria originally, and I went to college at William and Mary. I live with my best friend in Shirlington now, which is also where I work. I'm a librarian. And yes, Michelle, I'm on Instagram."

"Great. What about Snapchat?" Michelle asked.

Luke laughed and tousled Michelle's hair, which the young girl did not take kindly, too. "Let's let Lola catch her breath before we start cyber-stalking her. Gwen, can you grab Lola a drink, please? While you're at it, I'll take a beer."

With that, the crowd dispersed, although plenty of people stayed around Lola. She found she didn't mind. There were far too many questions and conversation for Lola to remember how nervous she'd been earlier.

As the only man in the pavilion, it had become his job to do the grilling, which he seemed to thoroughly enjoy. He did glance over at her from time to time with a question in his eyes. But each time she offered him a head nod or big smile to signify that she was doing just fine.

In fact, she was better than fine. She was enjoying chatting with everyone. Gwen made sure she had a beer, and Mia kept offering her chips, veggies, cookies, and more food. Winnie, who she was quickly learning was the sweetest of everyone in the family, kept complimenting her on everything from her glasses to her outfit—which made Lola sooo happy—to her toenail polish.

"Do you ever wear contacts?" Winnie asked.

"Come on, everyone. Food is ready. Let's eat," Aunt Sally called out.

As Lola made her way toward one of the picnic tables that they had covered with a large checkered tablecloth, she laughed. "No, I always wear my glasses. In fact, one time my roommate insisted I take my glasses off so I would look more attractive. I ended up spilling Jell-O all over your brother. It was so embarrassing."

"Did I hear embarrassing and brother?" Mia asked. "I must hear more."

They all took seats at the table that was piled with food. Everything from burgers and hot dogs to potato salad, macaroni salad, corn on the cob, chips, dip, large slices of watermelon, and Lola's fruit tray, covered the table. On a separate table there were about a million desserts, too. It smelled heavenly. The lingering charcoal smell gave the air that special aroma that screamed summertime.

"And you do not need to take your glasses off to look prettier," Winnie said to Lola. "I think you're gorgeous. Don't you agree, Ma?"

"Yes, I do. You hit the jackpot, Luke."

She glanced at Luke who had sat right next to her. His face was sporting quite the red glow.

"Are you blushing?" she whispered to him.

He shook his head. "It's just the heat from grilling."

"Yeah right," Mia said, leaning in from the other side.

Lola laughed. She'd been doing a lot of that today. Luke's family was great. They were so funny and welcoming. She felt like she'd known them forever.

She didn't know why she'd had such nerves coming into this.

She glanced across the table at Gwen, who was openly assessing her. "You're different than the other girls Luke has been interested in."

"Gwen!" Luke, Winnie, and Lorraine all said at the same time.

But Lola simply laughed. She was curious. "How so?" she asked Gwen.

"You're smart."

"Hey," Luke said.

"It's true," Mia added.

"And you have substance."

Lola didn't know what to say. She supposed it was as close to acceptance as she was going to get from Luke's toughest sister. Guilt settled in her stomach. She wondered what Gwen would think if she knew the truth, that this whole relationship was a facade.

Luckily, conversation picked up at the other end of the table. One of Luke's cousins had just graduated from high school, and everyone was excitedly discussing her upcoming plans to attend Virginia Tech in the fall.

About ten minutes later, Gwen put her burger down. "So, Lola, you've been Luke's secret girlfriend."

She choked on her hotdog. "Ugh, what?"

"It's just that Luke hasn't mentioned you at all. Not one little hint." Gwen threw a cocky smirk at her brother.

"I wanted to see where this was going first before I brought Lola around to meet this pack of hyenas," Luke said.

Luke squeezed her hand under the table. She relaxed.

"You two met online?" Aunt Sally asked.

"Yep, we met on a dating website," Lola said.

Gwen leaned forward on the table and peered at them. "You never told us you were on a dating website," she said accusingly.

Luke matched his sister's pose. "I don't tell you every single little thing that I do in life."

"It doesn't matter where they met. All that matters is that Lola is here now," Winnie said.

Luke was right. They were prepared. They'd talked about everything. Favorite television show from the early 2000s. Least favorite character in Harry Potter. Their favorite subject in elementary school.

"So, where did you two go on your first date?" Mia asked. *Oh. Holy. Shit.*

First date? They hadn't decided on a first date story. They'd nailed how they met, but it never occurred to her to think up a first date story.

They were both idiots. She could tell his family that Luke's favorite *Star Wars* movie was Episode IV or that he hated green beans, but not where they went on their first date. How could they not have planned for this?

"Uh," she stumbled. Panic rose in her throat. "Well, see, um, actually…"

Luke reached for her hand again and gave it a reassuring squeeze. She sneaked a glance at him, and his feathers didn't seem the tiniest bit ruffled.

"Actually," he began, "we went to this little Italian restaurant in Georgetown. On one of the side streets off M Street. They had the best damn eggplant parm I've ever eaten."

Her mouth fell open when she realized he was telling her parents' first date story, the one she'd revealed to him the other night. One of her absolute favorite memories. She rubbed a hand against her heart.

"Was it Ciao Bella on Wisconsin Avenue?"

"No. That place is a chain. Not very good. We went to Ristorante Formaggi. It's a tiny hole in the wall, but so delicious. Right, Lola?"

She blinked. What was it about Luke telling this story— or even remembering it at all—that had something fluttering in her stomach? It reminded her of all those times sitting around the dinner table when her mom and dad would make eye contact. A special glance would pass between them before one of them began the familiar story. "Oh yeah. The tablecloths looked like they were a hundred years old. Candles were placed everywhere and it smelled like—"

"Everything good about Italy. Basil and oregano and tomatoes and tiramisu," Luke finished.

Lola noticed Lorraine smile and then give a knowing nod to her sister.

"Lola had the gnocchi," Luke said. "She said it was almost as good as her grandmother's. Almost, but not quite."

"You listened," Lola said, her voice barely more than a whisper. As Luke relayed all of the minute details from the story she'd told him, her skin had started to tingle. "You listened to what I said." That fact made a world of difference.

Sure, her friends listened. Mostly. Honestly though, if an episode of *Real Housewives* was on, Lola knew Frankie's attention wouldn't be 100 percent.

"Of course I did. I listen to everything you say," Luke whispered back.

"Sounds yummy," Winnie said, oblivious to the emotion passing between her brother and Lola. "What did you have for dessert?"

"We split a cannoli," they said at the exact same time and laughed.

"Then we walked along the Potomac, past the Georgetown

waterfront and kept going until we reached—"

"The Lincoln Memorial," Lola finished this time. "The monuments are so beautiful at night. We sat on the steps and talked for hours."

Winnie let out a huge sigh. "Now there's a first date story. I wish I could find someone to share a story like that with."

"Hey, Erickson family."

Everyone turned to see an attractive man walking toward them. Lola thought he looked familiar. He wore a pair of khaki shorts, a light-green polo shirt, and the most wickedly handsome grin she'd ever witnessed.

Beside her, Winnie gasped. Lola was about to ask if she was okay, when Luke jumped up.

"Awesome. Oliver's here."

Everyone seemed to know Oliver. Lola learned that he and Luke had been best friends forever, so in a way he'd been part of the family for years. From Aunt Sally to Luke's cousins and his mother, everyone was thrilled Oliver showed up.

"You know I'd never miss an Erickson party."

Lorraine had already fixed a plate for him and was shooing him into a seat as she placed the loaded plate in front of him. Aunt Sally handed him a drink and gave him a kiss on the cheek.

She realized she had seen Oliver before. He'd been at Kennedy's High School reunion.

Yep, everyone seemed excited by this new arrival, except for one person. And didn't that just surprise the heck out of Lola.

She wanted to ask someone about it, but since she didn't know anyone well enough yet, she decided to keep her mouth shut. She could have asked Luke, but it seemed like he was utterly oblivious to the fact that fireworks practically went off any time his best friend and his sister Winnie exchanged glances.

Interesting.

They enjoyed their food. Then they took a break from eating, only to eat some more. Then another break ensued with a round of a fun card game. Then dessert was consumed.

Lola was pretty sure she'd never eaten so much food or had so much fun in one day. And that was before the water guns made an appearance.

When she'd first heard about these epic water battles, she didn't think she would be into it. But when the time came, she was happy to say that she was all over it. Not only that, but she was considered a fierce competitor. She even got Gwen good, which was apparently not the easiest task. She'd been given an Erickson round of applause for that one, which was followed up by Aunt Sally throwing a bucket of water at her. But everything had been in good fun. As Winnie threw her a towel and the two of them tried to salvage her hair, she overheard Luke talking to Mia.

"I don't know why you're so surprised," he said.

"I'm happily surprised. Never thought you would get over it and…"

Oliver began laughing loudly at something Lorraine said, and she missed the rest of the conversation, but it stayed with her. She was curious what Luke had gotten over.

A couple hours later after they helped clean up and load all of the cars, Lola retrieved her purse. The sun had set, and fireflies were making their appearance. An owl hooted in the distance.

Lorraine stopped her, shoving Tupperware at her.

"Here, some leftovers for you," she said with a smile.

"Thank you so much, Lorraine. For everything. I had a really great time today, and I'm so glad I met you all."

Guilt settled in the pit of her stomach. For the first time in hours, cold-hard reality came crashing down on her. She wasn't really Luke's girlfriend. She would probably never see any of these wonderful people again. Lorraine would never get her Tupperware back, and she'd be known as "that girl who crashed our reunion and stole our Tupperware." They would talk about her at Thanksgivings for years to come.

After all, she had made an agreement with Luke. Their fake relationship came to an end after tonight. She may never see him again, either. The thought gave her a sinking feeling in the pit of her stomach.

Maybe that was better anyway, she tried to rationalize. She and Luke were so different. He was a charming, sociable guy who liked to go out with his friends while she was much more content to stay in and watch a movie in her PJs. He was extroverted, and she was a clear introvert. He was a party animal, and she was a bookworm.

Yet somehow when their lips met, all of those differences disappeared.

Lola wanted to blow out a frustrated breath.

Lorraine offered a knowing look. "A million thoughts crossed your mind just now."

"Well…"

"Want to talk about it?" she asked softly, kindly.

"It's that…I mean to say…I had a really nice time today with you and your family," she said.

Lorraine stepped closer, cupped her cheek, and looked deeply in her eyes. Her mother used to do the same thing. Lola had to swallow down a huge lump in her throat.

"Luke told me about your parents, sweetie. I'm so sorry."

Tears threatened but Lola clamped down on those, too. "Thank you." Her voice was barely louder than a whisper.

"I understand your dad passed away when you were in high school."

Lola nodded. "He was in a bad car accident on the Beltway."

"How horrible." Lorraine was shaking her head. "And then your mother, too."

"It was ovarian cancer."

Concern coated Lorraine's face. Sadness, but not pity. "Was it a long struggle?"

"No, it was diagnosed late. There wasn't much time after that."

There could have been more time. Lola pushed the familiar anger to the back of her mind. Still, fragments of it remained. It always did.

"At least you were with her during that time."

Again, that anger threatened to boil up and explode. The truth was she hadn't been with her mom. Not the whole time; only at the very end. A decision that had been taken out of her hands. A lie that had been sustained as long as her mother could before Lola finally learned of the cancer.

Luke's loud laugh traveled over the warm summer air. He was messing around with Oliver and one of his cousins.

Maybe it wasn't such a bad thing that their pretend relationship was almost over. She knew from personal experience with her mom how much a lie could hurt. How it could damage a relationship and make a person feel unimportant.

Lorraine had been nothing short of wonderful today. Lola didn't want to hurt this woman. She didn't want to hurt anyone she'd met today. She would have to say goodbye to Luke tonight.

"I think you are a very strong woman, Lola." Lorraine squeezed her hands and then nodded firmly. "Now, onto other things. We're having a little cookout at my house next Saturday. It will be smaller than today's affair. Just the immediate family and some of their friends. I would love for you to come."

Hope swelled in her chest at the same time as regret

washed over her. "Really?" She would love nothing more than to hang out with Luke's family more. But she couldn't keep up with this lie. She just couldn't.

"Of course. I'm surprised Luke didn't invite you already." She wagged a finger at Lola. "I've seen the way my son looks at you."

"Really?" she repeated, this time with disbelief in her voice. "Oh, well, um…"

"I'll see you Saturday." Lorraine hugged her again.

What was she going to do now?

As she and Luke walked to his car, two things stuck out in her mind. One was how great Luke's family was. The other was something she had to bring up.

"What did your sister mean back there?"

"Which one?"

"Mia. She said you hadn't gotten over something."

He sighed and stopped walking. "It's stupid."

"What is it?"

"Just a thing about my dad leaving us. Mia believes that I'm not over it and I never will be. Blah, blah, blah. She loves therapy. Even though she's a baker, she likes to think she's a shrink."

Hm. Lola had a feeling that Mia was probably right on the money. From everything Luke had revealed to her, she had to admit it did sound like he had major daddy issues. Not that she blamed him one bit for them. After all, she had her own mommy issues to deal with.

They continued to the car. Luke held her door open and she slid in. He got behind the wheel and started the car, but he turned to her.

"Did you have fun today?"

"I did. It was…interesting."

"I hope my family wasn't too much of a pain in the ass."

"I think they're great. Really, really amazing."

"You do?"

She nodded. "I mean, it's great that you have them."

And it was. He had an amazing, wonderful, kind, loving family. Something that she didn't have. Something that she desperately wanted.

How great would it be to have kids one day and be able to bring them to something like this? Wouldn't it be wonderful to have traditions like the water fight? Or traditions at all.

She'd pretended to be someone's girlfriend today. That much she knew going into it. What Lola hadn't realized was that she'd also pretended to understand what it was like to be part of a big family.

But she didn't really know. She could only wish and hope and dream that someday she would get a family of her own.

Chapter Eight

"What kind of girl do you think I am? And how could you tell so fast."
-Blanche Devereaux

Luke had really enjoyed himself today. He always did when he was around his family. Sure, they were intrusive and nosy and kind of annoying. But when push came to shove, he knew that he was lucky as hell to have them.

Seeing Lola in that pavilion had been interesting. He hadn't anticipated how natural it would feel to watch her laugh with his sisters, hug his mother, and interact with his cousins.

At times, it had felt like she'd always been one of them.

He overheard his mom invite her to their barbeque the next week. That would be fun, too. They were also planning to go to King's Dominion in July. The whole family enjoyed amusement parks. He wondered if Lola did...

His thoughts trailed off as the gravity of what he'd been thinking sunk in. He was contemplating seeing Lola next week. Maybe even next month, too.

Then what? What would be next? Would he see her next year? In two years? Did he want that? Did she? It wasn't like they could keep this ruse up for that long. Besides, they weren't supposed to. The deal was that Lola would pretend to be his significant other until the end of his family reunion. When they got back in his car and drove out of the park, the reunion was officially over.

He snuck a peek at her as he drove through the streets of Arlington. Would she even want to go to the barbeque next week? And what was one week anyway? It wouldn't be a big deal to keep pretending for seven more days.

He shook his head. This had to stop. Which shouldn't be hard because it wasn't even real. She was his pretend girlfriend, and the jig was supposed to be up. Although, he did like hanging out with her. Maybe they could remain friends. He slipped a glance at her in the car. How would she feel about that? How would his family?

Damn, this had gotten way too complicated. And besides, Lola… He turned to her as he pulled up at a red light. That's when he realized something. Lola had been insanely quiet on the ride back. Eerily and completely silent.

He reached over and squeezed her hand. "Tired?" he asked.

She shook her head.

"Do you feel okay?" They'd all had a ton of food. His stomach was sure to start hurting at some point.

"I'm fine."

Uh-oh. A woman saying she was fine never boded well in his opinion, although he was glad she wasn't sick. He didn't know what to ask next. But he wanted to know what was wrong. He needed to know. Finally, Lola broke the silence.

"Don't you feel bad?"

"About what?"

"For deceiving your family. Your mom and sisters are so nice and you're…really lucky. You know, lucky to have them."

A pit formed in the center of his stomach as her words sunk in. Not only the words, but the meaning behind them. He felt like a first-rate insensitive idiot. He'd brought Lola to an event with a million family members. That had to bring up issues for her.

Luke wasn't sure what to say. How could he make this better for her? As he continued driving toward Lola's apartment he struggled to come up with something to say.

She angled toward him. "Your mom hugged me before we left. Really hugged me." Her voice broke.

"Lola?"

"It's nothing. I'm fine."

But clearly she wasn't. Luke was happy they'd reached her place. He didn't want to continue this conversation in the dark car.

He found a parking space across the street from her apartment building. Before he could even get his seatbelt unbuckled, Lola had opened her door and sprung from the car.

"You don't need to walk me inside."

"Lola, wait." Luke quickly exited the car, then ran back to grab the leftovers his mom had put together for her. He sprinted across the street. She was fast.

"Lola," he called again. When he reached her, he wrapped his fingers around her arm, forcing her to face him. His breath caught. Tears had pooled in her eyes.

"Hey," he said gently, "it's okay." He pulled her in for a hug, attempting to balance the leftovers as he did.

"You don't understand," she mumbled against his chest.

He realized she was right. Obviously, this was about her family, or lack thereof. How could he fathom what she went through? What she was still going through.

"Tell me," he whispered.

"I can't keep lying. I despise lying."

Luke nodded at a couple passing by on the sidewalk. They eyed Lola with concern, and he tried to convey that everything was okay. He pulled Lola to a bench next to the steps that led up to her building.

"I know lying is difficult for you. You're so sweet."

She made a sound that was somewhere between disgust and annoyance.

"But you are, Lola. You're one of the nicest people I've ever met."

She pushed a finger against his lips. "Shh. That's not it. I hate lying because of what a lie did to me when my mother was dying."

He froze. Out of all the things he expected her to say, bringing up her mother's death was definitely not one of them.

"What happened?" he asked.

She twisted her fingers together. "My mom was the worst about going to the doctor. She'd always make a joke about it or brush it off. To be fair, she didn't get sick very often. But still. My dad and I used to argue with her about going for a normal checkup. She was always so concerned about everyone else."

Lola closed her eyes, taking her time before she continued. Luke tried to give her the time she so obviously needed.

"She was diagnosed with ovarian cancer when I was in college. It was…too late." Her voice faltered.

"I'm so sorry, Lola." His words sounded hollow and inadequate. But it was all he could think to say.

She smiled briefly. "She didn't tell me about the cancer."

"What?"

"She didn't tell me. She was diagnosed with a fatal disease and given a very short time to live, and she kept it from me. Her only child. Her only living relative."

Oh holy shit. Luke couldn't believe what he was hearing. This certainly put a different slant on things.

"Every time I called from college, which was like every single day, she was all, 'I'm great, nothing to worry about.'" Lola shook her head. "I get it. I do. She didn't want me to worry, and she didn't want me to leave school."

"Would you have?"

An exasperated expression crossed her face. "Of course. I would have done anything to spend every single second with her that I could. But she took that away from me."

Lola ran a hand through her hair. "By the time I learned what was going on it was almost too late. I had two weeks with her. Two short weeks." Her gaze flicked up to meet his. "Do you know how hard it is to cram a lifetime of memories and love into a two-week goodbye?"

He tried to swallow down a large lump, but his throat had become very dry.

"I was angry. Really angry. But it wasn't like I could say that to my mom."

"So you've kept all that anger bottled up all these years?"

She shook her head. "Not really. I don't know. All I can say is that I realized back then how important it is to be honest, especially with the ones you love."

Luke felt like such an ass. "And here I've made you lie to my whole family." He stifled a groan.

Lola shrugged. "I went along with it. It's bothered me from the beginning, and I could have backed out at any minute, but I didn't."

"Why?"

She studied something on the ground. Her feet, her sandals, the sidewalk. Luke wasn't sure. Finally, he pressed. "Lola? Why did you go along with my plan if you're so against lying?"

"I guess because I wanted to be with you." She coughed

and bit her lip. "I mean, I wanted to get to know you."

He pulled in a deep breath at the admission.

Lola had hit him with such a myriad of information and feelings today. It had to be hard for her to be around his big, loud family, especially when she didn't have any family to speak of. Then, to learn more about her mother's cancer and her dislike of lying, really made his heart hurt for her.

Not to mention how he'd felt watching her with his family. How nice it was to see her interact with his sisters and mom. Now, having her admit that despite having a deep propensity against lying, she'd simply wanted to be with him, it was almost too much to take.

"Come on. Let's go inside." He took the key from her hand and let them in the outer door. They made their way to her apartment, and he unlocked that door as well.

Once they were inside, he put the leftovers away in the kitchen. When he returned to her, Lola was wringing her hands.

"Thanks for...well, thanks. You don't have to stay. I'm fine."

"No, you're not."

It was as if all the air left her body. She crumbled into a nearby chair. "It's hard to see such a big, loving family. To know that I don't have that."

She cast her eyes downward, and Luke's heart broke for her.

"You're not alone, Lola. You have Frankie and all your friends from bocce. You have your coworkers. And anyway, look at *The Golden Girls*."

Her gaze snapped up to meet his with a distinct are-you-kidding-me expression. "Oh no. Not that again. Have you been talking to Frankie?"

"Well, she followed me on Instagram and Snapchat. She snapped the two of you watching an episode the other night."

Lola sighed. "She's ridiculous."

"Hey, it's a pretty good show. Ahead of its time."

"What do you know about it anyway?"

"I used to watch it with my grandma," he said proudly.

She sighed. "Me too. What's your point?"

"But it's been years so I started watching it again. Frankie sent me some of her favorite episodes. My point is that *The Golden Girls* made their own family. Dorothy, Rose, Blanche, and Sophia weren't related."

"Dorothy and Sophia were."

"Stepping on my point here. The rest weren't related, and they didn't let that small detail stop them from being a family."

He saw her acceptance of his point. But she remained silent. He crouched in front of her chair. Grabbed her hands.

"I repeat, you have Frankie, the bocce league, your coworkers. And you have me."

Behind her glasses, her brows furrowed. "Do I?"

"Yes."

"I thought you didn't get close to people."

"I don't."

"Then what are you doing?"

What *was* he doing? He just told her that he didn't get close to people, and yet that was the one thing he wanted to do with her.

"With you, I can't seem to stop myself. I try to put a wall up, and I find myself wanting you more."

She stood up. "This isn't going to end well."

Probably not. But right now, Luke couldn't think further than the end of tonight.

"I can leave," he said, but even as he did, he stepped closer to her.

Lola closed the distance between them. "I don't want you to leave," she whispered.

He gulped. His heart was pounding hard, reverberating throughout his body. Even after the long day, the heat, the water battle, he could still smell her intoxicating scent. Her chest was rising and falling, beckoning him to focus his attention there.

"What do you want?"

She fiddled with her glasses before meeting his gaze. Strongly, confidently, she said, "I want you."

That was all he needed to hear. Luke grabbed her and crushed his mouth to hers. Finally, he was getting what he'd craved all day long.

The kiss was heated and heavy, soaking into his very being. He felt sated in a way he never had before.

Luke told Lola multiple times that he didn't do relationships. But when she kissed him like this, it was hard to remember that tiny detail.

• • •

Lola didn't think. She allowed herself to feel and to enjoy.

And what a thing to enjoy.

Luke was kissing her wildly, and she was meeting him beat for beat. She fisted her hands in his shirt, yanking him closer to her. She wanted to feel him. All of him. Was he as dizzy as she was? Was his pulse hammering away?

Suddenly, he stopped kissing her. "Frankie," he mumbled against her lips.

Lola pulled back. "You know, I'm not too picky. But calling out another girl's name while you're kissing me might be my limit, especially when it's my roommate."

He grinned. "Sorry. I was just checking. Is Frankie home?"

"What?" Relief washed over her. "Oh no, she went to the beach for the weekend. She won't be back until late tomorrow night."

"We're alone then?" His eyes darkened.

She bit her lip and nodded. "Yep."

The implication was out there. It was just the two of them, and need hung heavily in the air around them. They were going to do way more than kiss tonight.

It wasn't like Luke was the first guy she'd been with. Lola had been dating since high school. Yet, nerves swirled around her.

"Come here," he said, his voice husky.

Despite his words, Luke didn't make a move, either. Maybe he was nervous, too. The two of them stayed like that, staring at each other. Their chests were rising and falling, and the air around them had thickened with the anticipation of lust and longing.

Suddenly, as if the spell had been broken, they reached for each other. More like hungrily grabbed for each other.

Their mouths fused together. Her lips parted, and he took advantage by plunging his tongue inside. She ran her hands up his back and into his hair. She pulled him closer to her, knowing that she could never get enough. Never.

Someone moaned and for the life of her, Lola had no idea who it was. Didn't care.

On a shaky breath, she said, "Should we move this to my bedroom?"

"Yes," he said against her lips. "God, yes."

They began walking, their mouths still devouring each other, their hands still grasping for any skin they could find. They made it a couple steps before they tripped. Luke landed in the oversize chair, pulling her with him. Lola was only too happy to take advantage of the position. She straddled him, immediately reaching for his belt. Her fingers skimmed the sensitive skin just above his pant line, and Luke sucked in a harsh breath.

As she undid the belt and began working the button and zipper of his pants, she moved her lips along the column of his throat. He smelled so good. Whatever cologne he wore smelled like rugged man, all musky and masculine.

When she nipped his earlobe, he bucked. Lola chuckled. She couldn't help it. "You like that?"

"Just a bit."

She realized she still had her glasses on. She raised her hand to remove them, but Luke's hand covered hers.

"No, leave them."

"My glasses?" She scrunched her nose.

"Oh, hell yes. They have to stay."

With that, he locked his arms around her bottom and stood, bringing her with him. Momentarily stunned that he could lift her as if she weighed no more than a stack of books, she clung to him. Then she wrapped her legs around his waist as he began to walk toward the bedrooms.

Her mouth found his again. The kiss went deep. His taste was intoxicating, and she knew she could kiss him forever. She did a little trick she'd learned at summer camp where she circled her tongue around his. He stopped walking as he shivered and moaned. One of his hands came up to the back of her head, encouraging her to keep doing her little tongue trick. She was only too happy to oblige.

After teasing him for a long time as they stood in the middle of the living room, he grunted. "Remind me which bedroom is yours."

"You were in it this morning," she said on a laugh.

"Right now, with your legs wrapped around me like that, I couldn't tell you my own name."

In that case… "It's the one on the left. No, the other left," she said as he began moving again.

The next thing she knew, her back hit something hard, and there was a crash. The wall. She was in the hallway outside the bedrooms, against the cool wall as Luke's body plastered against her. One of the framed photos she and Frankie had put up had fallen at the force. Oh well, she'd deal with that later.

Luke released her legs, and she touched the carpet with her toes. She couldn't wait anymore. They were close enough to the bedroom. She yanked his pants down. As they pooled around his feet, she took a peek. Black boxer briefs that were more than a little filled out. In fact, they were bursting with his need. Yum.

She grinned as her hands cupped his firm ass and gave a little squeeze. He was busy doing something wonderful to her neck. Her fingers made their way around his body until they snuck under the band of his underwear. When her hand found him, she gasped. He was long and thick and hard.

She wrapped her hand around his length with just the right pressure. Luke made a sound like a growl and wrenched her shirt to the side.

Had it just ripped? Whatever, she didn't care, especially when his mouth found her breast. Even through her lacy bra, the sensation of his warm mouth had her nipple hardening into a tight little bud. She threw her head back as he continued to suck her into his mouth.

The rubbing of the lace against her puckered nipple was too much. She quickly unhooked her bra and threw it to the side.

"There," she said triumphantly to Luke.

He grinned. "Thanks for the help." And then his mouth was fused to her other breast.

He bit and sucked and kissed and nipped, and Lola thought her legs would turn into a puddle of mush on the floor. Good thing she was trapped between Luke's hard body and the cold wall.

She threw her head back as far as the wall would allow,

letting herself accept all of the pleasure Luke was giving her. She felt his hand travel down over her stomach, eliciting a small *whoosh* of breath as he passed over her ticklish spot. Then it kept going until it reached the waistband of her leggings.

His clever fingers wasted no time moving lower until they were under her pants and circling her panties. Next thing she knew Luke had cupped her. His mouth moved from her breast to kiss her long and soundly as his hand stayed steady covering her center. He was much more patient than she was, and she let him know that by letting out a full moan into his mouth. She thought she heard him chuckle in triumph, or maybe that was her imagination. But when he took the opportunity to push his tongue into her mouth at the same time as one of his fingers slid inside of her, she didn't care who was winning.

His tongue mirrored what his finger was doing between her legs. In and out, in and out. Lola arched her back against the wall, trying and failing to steady herself. Then Luke pushed a second finger inside her, and she knew she was close to losing it completely.

"Luke," she murmured against his lips.

"Yes," he answered. "That's it. Come for me, baby."

If she must. Lola closed her eyes and let the overwhelming sensation of pleasure wash over her as her body emptied into Luke's waiting hand.

He made a purely male sound. A sound of satisfaction. Then his hands were at her hips and those fingers once again became busy wrapping around her waistband. In one fast, fluid movement, Luke yanked both her leggings and panties down to the floor. She obliged him by stepping out of them.

She felt his mouth on her legs, as he laid gentle kisses over every inch of her. First one leg, then the other, starting at her calves and moving up to nip at her knees. His tongue licked at her thighs, as his hands came around to explore the shape of her ass.

He traveled all the way up to the vee of her legs, which was pulsing with need, with want, with a yearning to release the most exquisite of pleasures. His mouth covered her, and she bucked against the wall. Her hands went to his head, trying to grab his hair. But he had a short cut and that wouldn't work. As his tongue flicked out to tease her, she clasped on to his head, holding him against her wanton pussy.

She felt a vibration and realized he was doing something beyond amazing with his lips. She gripped his head tighter. My God, she was going to suffocate him, but she couldn't worry about that now as his tongue was darting in and out of her center, causing stars to form behind her eyes.

She was close, very close, yet torn about whether she wanted this delicious pleasure to end giving her what was sure to be an earth-shattering release or if she wanted Luke to stay just like that, doing just that, for the rest of her days.

When his finger pressed against her nub, she knew the decision was out of her hands. She couldn't hold on any longer. His name ripped from her lips in a loud moan as she came.

Spent, she willed her breathing to slow down, but she was helpless to do anything but lean against the wall and wait for Luke's next attack. He immediately complied by trailing feather-soft kisses across her stomach. His hands were busy exploring every inch of her.

"You're so soft." He leaned his head back, and she looked down to see him lick his lips. "So sweet."

He fondled her breasts again, but gently, so gently. Then his mouth covered one and he pulled her taut nipple into his mouth, sucking hard. He stood, returning to her mouth, leaning in for what was sure be another hot kiss, but Lola stopped him with a finger to his mouth. "Uh-uh," she said.

"Your turn." She reached down and plucked the waistband of his boxer briefs, pulling and let them gently snap back. "I think you deserve some attention now."

He shook his head and bit her lower lip. "Nope. Baby, if you go down there I won't be able to make it. And I need to be inside of you. Now."

He leaned over and grabbed something out of his pants pocket. She recognized the foil wrapper. He ripped it with his teeth, shoved his boxer briefs to the floor, and quickly covered himself.

"Are you ready?" he asked, his voice sounding deeper than she'd ever heard it.

His eyes had gone dark with need. Want for her.

"Yes," she said. "Oh yes."

She felt the tip of his penis at her center. His arm came out and wrapped around one of her legs, yanking it around his waist.

There was a brief moment, where they stood like that, eyes boring into each other. They were naked and about to be joined in every way possible. Right there, in the hallway of her apartment.

Lola should feel embarrassed, but she didn't. She should feel exposed. Instead, she felt more wanted than she had in her entire life.

"What do you want, Lola?"

She didn't have to think twice. "I want you inside of me. Now, Luke, now."

With that, he pushed into her, wrenching a moan from her trembling lips. He sighed deeply and kissed her.

"Are you okay, baby?"

She took stock of her body, allowing it a moment to accommodate his considerable size. "Yes." The word was half spoken, half moaned.

He began to move inside her. One arm still held her leg,

the other was braced against the wall next to her head. He pulled out slowly, torturously. She thought he was going to exit her body completely, then at the last possible moment, he slammed back into her, hard. Then he repeated the movement over and over again. Slide out gently, slowly. Push back in with such force as to make her legs weak. It was a decadent combination between massive pleasure and exquisite pain.

"Luke, yes."

He began to move faster then. She tried to meet him thrust for thrust, but she was positioned at an awkward angle.

As if reading her mind, Luke reached down and grabbed her other leg. She gasped. She was wrapped around him, her body spread open to him in every way.

He pushed into her with reckless abandon, her back slamming against the wall. A sheen of sweat had begun to bead on his skin, but Lola did her best to hang on, her arms twined tightly around his shoulders. Her nails were digging into his back as he fucked her thoroughly and completely.

"Lolaaaaa," he screamed as he rammed himself into her.

She'd never been taken like this before. It was as if Luke couldn't get enough of her. Like she was driving him as mad as he was driving her.

He was losing it. She could tell. But then again, so was she. How could she climax for a third time in such a short period of time? There was no time to think on that as her body began to tremble, her pussy clenching around his warm, hard cock.

She panted his name over and over.

"Yes, baby, come for me again."

Without hesitation, she did. Her body shook, and she let out a guttural moan that she'd never heard before. Then with one final move, Luke pushed her against the wall, his fingers tightening around her legs as he experienced his own release.

Lola's arms fell loosely, limply, from Luke's shoulders.

She felt the wall. Thank God it was still there. She wouldn't have been surprised if they had dislodged it.

After what transpired between them, Lola knew that everything she had held onto had been dislodged.

• • •

Luke woke to the most wonderful feeling. Something soft and smooth was up against him. A scent of sweet flowers surrounded him.

That something shifted and let out a cute little half sigh, half yawn.

Lola.

He was spooning her. She was on her side with her backside up against him. His arm was anchored over her waist. He ran a hand up her arm.

The sunlight was streaming through her window. He took a minute to observe her bedroom. They sure hadn't had time for that last night, what with him taking her up against the wall, on the bed, at the end of the bed, on the chair in the corner. They'd loved each other in every way possible, and his body was feeling heavy and sated now. He wanted to let out a contented yawn and stretch his arms high over his head. But he also didn't want to wake Lola since they hadn't fallen asleep until very late.

He pulled the white comforter with blue flowers over her since he could feel the AC kick on again. The sheets on her bed were a basic white, but there was an array of throw pillows scattered across the floor in varying shades of blue, from baby to navy to turquoise. They picked up all the hues in her comforter and also matched the curtains on the two windows in the room. Her furniture was white, and very girly lamps with feathers stood on them, along with a couple books.

He recalled she'd said last night that she had the bigger bedroom in the apartment and he could tell that now. At the end of the bed, there was room for a large dresser with a big oval mirror hung above it. To the left, there was a matching bookshelf, crammed to the gills with books of various sizes and shapes. There were also picture frames. He noticed Frankie and some of the other girls he'd met at her bocce game.

On the end table closest to him, there was a beautiful black frame with the word *FAMILY* embossed on it in silver. Lola was smiling at him from the photo. She was much younger, but still adorable. She wore different glasses than she had now. They were thinner, made of little gold frames. A man and a woman had their arms around her, and there was a Christmas tree in the background.

Her parents. A lump formed in his stomach. It was still hard to believe that she had no family left in the world. Luke couldn't fathom it. They'd had such a great time with his the day before. Until, of course, Lola had grown sad in the car. And wasn't that how he'd ended up in her bed?

His arm tightened around her protectively. He nuzzled her neck, and she let out another adorable sound. Did it matter how or why he'd woken up here? He'd wanted her last night. Badly. He'd wanted her since the first time he met her when she was wearing that uncharacteristically sexy dress at his reunion.

He didn't do relationships, but this wasn't a relationship. Not yet, anyway. They'd had fun last night. Fun and mind-blowing sex. He grew hard again just thinking about it.

He wanted her again. Right here, right now. Did he need to analyze that? He could just live in the moment. Take it day by day.

But could she?

Luke didn't want to hurt her. Then again, she was a big

girl, and she'd entered into last night willingly. Then there was no more time to think about it, because Lola yawned, her eyelids fluttering open. She took a moment to orient herself with the new day and the body still fit snug around her own.

She rolled to face him, rubbing against his ready appendage as she did. Her eyes grew wide. "Well, good morning to you."

He kissed the tip of her nose. "Yes, it is good."

She laughed and kissed him deeply. She let out a purr against his lips. "I can't believe that, um, thing down there," she said, casting her eyes toward his now-throbbing penis, "is so eager already."

"Oh, he's a spry little guy."

"I'll attest to that, but I would have thought he'd be tired after such an energetic night."

Luke ran his fingers through her hair. It was tousled and messy. Her makeup was smeared under her eyes. She was the sexiest thing he'd ever seen.

"Nah," he said. "It's a whole new day. Speaking of, you said Frankie wouldn't be home until later tonight?"

She smiled. "She's at Dewey Beach for the weekend. With all that beach traffic coming back into the city, she probably won't get home until really late."

"That means you have the whole apartment to yourself."

"For the entire day."

"What will you do with all that freedom?" he asked, inching his hand down her body.

"Hm, I don't know. Any suggestions?" She shoved at him gently until he was on his back. Then she climbed on top of him, her hair falling over her shoulders, blanketing her face in the sexiest way.

"I think I might have a few."

With that, he began to show her exactly what he had in mind.

Chapter Nine

"I'm not one to blow my own vertubenflugen."
-Rose Nylund

Best. Week. Ever.

Lola couldn't stop smiling. Even her coworkers had noticed. Of course, she didn't want to admit the source of her happiness was a handsome hottie sharing her bed almost every night this week. Instead, she'd explained that she was simply happy it was Friday.

Unfortunately, she wouldn't be able to see Luke tonight. She and Frankie were at Olivia's house for a girls' night featuring wine, cheese, and some old Disney movies. They liked to do this once a month or so. Tonight's double feature was *Beauty and the Beast* and *Aladdin*.

Lola looked at the DVD cover for *Aladdin*. Seems she didn't need a genie. She was fulfilling lots of wishes this week all on her own.

Well, Luke was helping with that.

He'd joined them for bocce again on Monday night.

They'd hung out with Frankie on Tuesday and watched a movie at their apartment. Wednesday and Thursday she'd gone to his place. They'd ordered food and stayed in. She could feel herself blushing as she thought about what "staying in" meant for them.

She should be tired. But Lola felt great, energized, excited about, well, everything. She was especially looking forward to seeing Luke's family again tomorrow at their barbeque. A huge difference from the week before when she'd been anxious and dreading attending their family reunion.

She put the DVD back on Olivia's TV stand. Olivia shared a small town house with Summer in Old Town Alexandria. Unfortunately, the whole bocce team couldn't make it tonight, but it was unusual for all eight of them to be free for a girls' night at the same time.

Since they were still waiting for Lanette and Hannah to arrive, Lola snagged a carrot stick and dipped it in Summer's homemade hummus that they all loved. As she was chewing, Frankie sidled up to her.

"Hm, what?" Lola asked. She'd been thinking about Luke again.

Frankie frowned. "I asked what you were thinking about."

"Oh nothing." She took her cell out of her pocket and shot Luke a quick text.

Thinking of you. What are you doing tonight?

He wasted no time replying.

I know what I wish I was doing…

Be good, she replied.

My sister is coming over to watch a movie, aka, torment me.

Lola smiled. *Tell her I said hi.*

As she put her phone away, she noticed that Frankie was staring at her, her brows drawn together.

"What's with the look?" Lola asked.

Frankie's answer was a long sigh.

Frankie had been acting strange about her and Luke for a couple days now. She would have thought Frankie would be happy about the two of them since she was the one who basically got them together. Not to mention that if Lola hadn't taken her *Golden Girls* advice in the first place, she would have never met Luke. So what was her problem?

She silently chastised herself. Frankie was her best friend. She'd been there for Lola through breakups and different jobs and pretty much every issue that had come up in her life. Not to mention she'd been Lola's rock during her mom's death. Without Frankie, Lola had no idea how she would have gotten out of bed during that time. Her best friend deserved more patience than she was giving her right now.

"Is everything okay?" Lola asked.

"You've spent a ton of time with Luke this week," Frankie said bluntly.

Lola felt her defenses go up. "So what?"

Frankie's face fell. "I'm just saying."

Lola felt like a jerk. Maybe she'd been spending a little too much time with Luke. Maybe Frankie felt left out. Oh no. She didn't want to alienate her best friend. After all, she'd watched plenty of friends fall fast and hard into relationships, leaving their other friends behind in the dust. That never felt good.

Olivia breezed through the living room then carrying paper plates and plastic cups.

"Do you guys need any help?" Frankie asked Olivia.

Olivia shook her head. "Nope, all good. Celeste is fixing drinks, Summer ran out for more ice, and I'm gonna order the pizza now."

"Great. Lo and I are gonna chat on your lanai."

Olivia laughed. "Most people call it a patio, you know."

"At Blanche's house, it's a lanai," Frankie said knowingly.

Lola had to stifle an eye roll. More *Golden Girls*. Frankie was ridiculous. She called every outdoor space a lanai.

Frankie grabbed Lola's hand and drew her outside onto the tiny brick-covered patio off the dining room. As soon as they stepped out into the summer heat, the sounds of Old Town surrounded them. Traffic and car horns mixed with laughter as people made their way toward the plethora of restaurants and bars in Alexandria's trendy neighborhood.

Lola shook Frankie's firm grasp. "What gives?" she asked as Frankie closed the door and faced her with worried eyes.

"You stayed at Luke's last night."

Lola didn't know how to respond. It wasn't a question, but Frankie was waiting for her to say something. "Yeah, I told you that's where I would be."

Frankie crossed her arms over her chest. "You stayed there the whole night."

She hadn't meant to, but they'd been kind of busy, and when they realized the time, Luke suggested she just stay.

Frankie was waiting again, her expression morphing into something that was borderline mad.

"Why are you looking at me like that?"

"Why are you spending the entire night with a guy you've only known a couple weeks? Hooking up is one thing but actually sleeping over? That's kind of intense."

Lola ran her hands through her hair. "I thought you liked Luke."

"I do. It's just that..." Frankie trailed off, twisting her hands together.

"What?"

"You *really* like him."

"Yeah?" Lola wanted to scratch her head. Frankie wasn't making any sense.

Lola took a moment. She wasn't sure where this

conversation was going or what it was even about. Stalling for time, she paced the small patio, checking out the almost-dead plant in a pot on the small table. Olivia couldn't keep a plant alive to save her life.

"I'm worried about you, Lo."

"Why? Because I'm seeing a guy? You see guys all the time."

Frankie remained silent, her face set tightly, giving away nothing.

"I mean, didn't you have a date last night, too?"

Nodding, Frankie remained quiet. The silent treatment was killing Lola.

"Plus, you have a ton of guy friends, and you're always talking to someone or texting with some hottie."

Frankie sighed. The first sound she'd made. "Lola, I have a ton of guy friends, because I work with all men."

It was true. Frankie was a computer programmer and one of the few women in her company. Not to mention that she was also incredibly outgoing, and people just naturally wanted to be around her.

"And I go out with a lot of different people because that's my personality. I'm extroverted and I put myself out there. Plus, I enjoy being social and hanging with different people." She pointed at Lola. "You're not like that."

"Are you saying something's wrong with me?" Lola asked.

Frankie rushed to her side and took her hand. "No, of course not. I'm just worried," she repeated.

"There's nothing to be concerned over. Everything's going great. I'm heading over to Luke's mom's house tomorrow for a barbeque."

Frankie pointed at her. "See, right there. Your face is glowing."

"Is that a bad thing?"

"I date a lot of different guys because I enjoy dating. But it's rarely serious. I'm okay with that." She paused and bit her lip before continuing. "Luke is awesome, but he doesn't want a relationship, Lola. He's told you that."

"Well, I know he said that, but—"

"But nothing. You don't want to be one of *those* girls."

"What girls?" Lola asked.

"You know." Frankie sighed. "Those girls who go into a relationship with their eyes wide open. But it doesn't matter. They think they can change their partner."

Lola wanted to groan. What was Frankie talking about? She offered a blank stare.

"Like, if you got married knowing your husband didn't want to have kids. But you think that you can wear him down. Change him."

"Um, Luke and I are not getting married or talking about kids."

"I know, I know. You're missing the point."

Lola nodded emphatically. "I'm totally missing it."

"From what you've told me, Luke has some legitimate intimacy issues from his dad leaving the family. That's understandable. And you want a family. A husband and kids and the whole white picket fence."

"That's not a crazy thing to want," Lola mumbled.

Frankie moved closer. "No, of course it's not."

"And you were the one who pushed me to go out. Pushed me to meet someone new. Pushed me toward Luke."

Frankie shook her head ferociously. "No, I didn't. I pushed you toward a no-strings-attached one-night stand. Or a quick fling. Just a little rebound guy." She frowned. "I messed up. Because you are not the type of girl who can do that."

"Frankie—"

"No, this is all my fault. I only wanted you to get over the hurt of stupid Mark dumping you. Now you're going to get hurt all over again. Probably worse than with Mark."

"What are you talking about?"

"This whole thing between the two of you was supposed to be pretend. You were supposed to be his fake girlfriend for his family reunion."

"So what?"

"The reunion was last weekend. Why are you still pretending?"

"Well, uh, his mom invited me to the barbeque while we were at the reunion last week."

"You could have said no."

"That would have been rude."

Frankie bit her lip. Then she hugged Lola tightly. "You're not pretending anymore, Lola. That's the problem. You've developed feelings for Luke, and they aren't fake."

"Maybe Luke has developed feelings for me, too. Have you ever thought of that?"

She nodded. "Sure. He'd be crazy not to."

"Then what's the problem?"

"I know Luke's type. I kind of am Luke's type, in female form," she mumbled. "I don't want him to use you."

Lola felt like Frankie had slapped her. "Use me? For what?"

"Oh, Lola." Frankie paced a couple steps away. "For sex."

Olivia stuck her head out the door then. "Hey, you guys ready for some vino and Disney? Lanette and Hannah just got here."

"We'll be there in a sec." Frankie turned back to Lola, reaching for her hand and squeezing. "I'm so sorry, Lola."

She wanted to be mad but she couldn't, especially when she saw the earnestness in Frankie's eyes. "You're looking out for me. I'd do the same for you."

"I know you would." She started to walk inside.

"Coming?"

"I'll be there in a sec. I'm fine, Frankie," she said when Frankie paused with her hand on the doorknob. "Really."

Lola's head was spinning. She heard what her best friend said. Loud and clear. Her brain took in all that information. The problem was that her heart didn't.

Her phone went off in her pocket. She pulled it out and saw a text from Luke.

Can't wait to see you tomorrow.

She crossed to the table, sat down, and put her head in her hands. Frankie was right. Luke had told her he didn't want a relationship. Their pretend relationship was only supposed to last for one day and that day happened last week. But she couldn't ignore this week. All the time spent with Luke.

Frankie was wrong.

It hadn't been just sex. They talked. A lot. They ate together. He came to their rogue bocce game, for God's sake. If he wanted a hookup, he would do what all the other guys did. She'd get a text message late at night asking what she was up to. She wouldn't sleep over at his place. He wouldn't buy her favorite beer for her and have it waiting at his house. They wouldn't exchange texts and snaps throughout the day.

They wouldn't be okay with you joining their family at a damn barbeque.

Then there was everything they'd shared with each other. Besides Frankie, Luke was the only other person she'd ever told about her mom keeping the cancer from her. And Luke had confided in her about his dad. How he left Luke's family and never looked back.

What kind of guy would reveal such a personal detail? Certainly not one who was only in it for sex.

Lola really wanted to see his mom and sisters again. She'd enjoyed spending time with them so much. Spending time with a real family who laughed and fought and teased each other.

She loved the way his mom would hug her snugly. It had felt great to have his sisters include her in their jokes and stories. The entire family had embraced her as if she really was a part of it. But she wasn't part of it. She didn't have a family. The words Luke had spoken to her after his family reunion came back to her. She did have a family. Frankie and her friends were there for her.

At least, for now. Most of her friends were still single. What happened as they started finding people of their own? Serious relationships that led to marriage and kids? What was she supposed to do then?

Her stomach sank. Even though she hadn't had any food in her stomach since lunch, she felt like she was going to be sick. The prospect of a long, lonely life was enough to have a headache start brewing.

The door opened, and Summer stuck her head out. "Everything okay, Lola?"

She jumped up. "Yeah, sorry. I was checking a text message."

"Then get in here. Frankie is going to eat all the chips and guac. Just like she did last time."

"I heard that," Frankie yelled from inside the house. "I did not eat all of it last time."

"She totally did," Summer whispered as Lola joined her and walked into the house.

"Totes," she agreed.

As her friends enjoyed the wine and cheese, Lola tried to have fun, but her heart wasn't in it. All that yummy food tasted stale in her mouth. She'd lost her appetite.

While she tried to laugh at her friends' jokes and keep up with a conversation about the latest episode of *The Bachelorette*, her mind kept drifting. Right over to Luke Erickson.

She really didn't want to admit it but Frankie was right. Luke didn't want a girlfriend or a relationship. She'd known that going into this. Yet here she was about to get hurt.

As they settled in to watch a little Disney magic, her spirits couldn't help but be lifted. Maybe this was her princess moment. Maybe she'd found her prince like Belle and Jasmine.

She decided to stop wallowing. Everything would turn out all right in the end.

Now if she could only believe her own words.

• • •

"Lola's here."

Lola smiled as she entered Luke's mother's house hand in hand with him the next morning.

"I'm here, too," Luke said indignantly.

"Who cares about you?" Gwen said as she rounded the corner and punched him in the shoulder. "Hey, Lola."

"Hi, Gwen."

Winnie came bouncing out of the kitchen. "Lola!" she exclaimed. She stopped and tilted her head as she took in their joined hands. "Awww, I don't think I've ever seen Luke hold hands with a girl before."

"I've seen him hold hands with a guy." Mia joined them from another room. "Remember how scared you and Oliver were when we watched *The Blair Witch Project*?" she said in a childlike voice.

Luke rolled his eyes. "We were ten. Can you please get over that?"

Mia snorted. "No way."

"I've got pictures of it," Gwen said, returning. "Wanna see, Lola?" She smirked.

"You're dead." Luke released Lola's hand and ran after

his sister.

"What is with all this yelling? Oh, Lola, sweetheart, you're here." Lorraine came down the stairs and embraced Lola in one of those great hugs.

"I brought some wine for you. Luke said this is your favorite." Lola held out the bottle of white wine and the Tupperware she'd borrowed the week before.

"You don't need to bring something every time I see you. But thank you. It is my favorite. Come on into the kitchen. Or the zoo as I like to call it."

Lola followed her through a hallway lined with what were surely family pictures. She wanted to get a closer look later. The house was beautiful. It sat on a tree-lined street in North Arlington, at the end of a cul-de-sac. It was painted white with green shutters and a matching front door. Plants and flowers decorated the brick walkway and hydrangea sat under the front windows.

From what she'd seen so far, the inside was just as welcoming. It looked like there was a living room on one side of the foyer and a dining room on the other. The end of the hallway she was walking down opened up into a large kitchen, done all in white with blue and gray granite counters and back splash. It reminded Lola of her mother's kitchen. Only this one had a large counter that separated it from a cozy family room with a fireplace and lots of windows and French doors. She saw a pool outside, the blue water sparkling in the warm summer sun. Luke had told her to bring her bathing suit. There was a well-kept patio, large grill, tables, chairs, and more flowers.

She did a little turn. What a great house.

"What do you think?" Luke asked, even as he had Gwen in a loose headlock.

"It's wonderful. So this is your childhood home?"

"The one and only," Mia said. "By the way, I ran into

Oliver in Clarendon last night. He's coming over."

Again, Lola noticed Winnie's face pale. She promptly grabbed a basket with paper plates, utensils, and napkins and went out to the patio. Interesting.

"Great," Lorraine said. "Luke, why don't you give Lola a tour of the house?" The doorbell rang. "That's probably your aunt now. Mia, take these out to Winnie." She handed something over.

"I'll get it," Gwen yelled and ran for the door.

"Welcome to Grand Central," Luke said, taking Lola's hand again. "It tends to be chaotic twenty-four-seven around these parts, especially when we're all home. You should see it at Christmas."

Her heart clenched. How she would love to see it at the holidays. She could imagine that Lorraine would have every inch of the house decorated with twinkly lights and decorations that had been in the family for ages. Luke and his sisters probably rushed around yelling at each other and snagging food, just as they were now. Homey aromas of cinnamon and spices probably emanated from the kitchen.

Yes, she'd very much like to witness that.

"Come on." Luke tugged on her hand and pulled her out of her thoughts.

He showed her the backyard and pool area. When they walked back down the hallway, she made him stop and explain each of the framed photos on the wall. They had a pretty killer game room set up in the finished basement with an enormous television, a pool table, air hockey, and a bar in one corner.

"This is amazing. I bet you guys had so much fun down here when you were in high school."

"Oh, we did," Luke said. "I think my mom had the basement refinished for the specific purpose of getting us out of her hair. We'd all gather down here with our friends, and mom would stay upstairs with her book and enjoy some peace and quiet."

They walked up to the second floor. Luke pointed out his mom's room and the large bedroom his sisters had shared. She peeked in and saw three twin beds were still positioned around the room. Above each bed where posters and other decorations. Funny how each of his sisters had a completely different personality. Winnie was the sweet, girly-girl while Gwen was her polar opposite and definitely the most badass of the three. Mia sat somewhere in between with a touch of practicality.

"And this is my room. Well, it was my room." Luke ushered her inside.

Lola walked around, getting a feel for the place. It was much smaller than his sister's room. But he had a double bed, a dresser, desk, closet. All the usual stuff.

"Nice bean bag chair," she noted with a grin.

"It's a necessity for game playing."

"Your room is very…masculine." The furniture was a dark wood, and his bedding and curtains were navy blue.

"My mom keeps saying she's going to turn our bedrooms into different things like a scrapbooking room and a gym, but she never does. Every time we come home, our stuff is still exactly where we left it."

Must be nice, she thought. A lot of her stuff from high school and most of the furniture and belongings from her parents' house was now in storage. Someday she would have a house of her own and get everything back out.

Luke's arms came around her from behind, snaking around her waist. He moved her hair to the side, his mouth nuzzling her neck.

"Mmm," she moaned. "That feels…wrong!"

Luke's head snapped up. "What?"

"You can't do that to me. Not here."

He spun her around. "Why not?"

Was he crazy? "We're in your mother's house." She over exaggerated each word, speaking very slowly.

"So?" He closed the door, flicking the lock. Then he crossed back to her, backing her up until her legs bumped the edge of his bed.

"Luke, what are you doing?"

He ran his fingertips up her arm, grazing her breasts as he did. Then he placed a kiss at the left edge of her mouth, then the right. Finally, he took her lips in a sultry kiss that had her legs buckling.

"What do you think I'm doing?" he said against her lips.

She pushed back. "Oh, I think I can figure it out. But you have to stop."

He covered one breast with his large hand. Through the thin material of the red tank top she wore, she could feel the heat from his hand. He caressed her. Her nipples hardened, and he pinched one.

"You really want me to stop?" he asked with a cocky grin.

He knew damn well she didn't, especially when he began feasting on her neck and her head fell back. "But…but…your mother, your sisters…downstairs." She closed her eyes and moaned.

He took advantage of the opportunity to gently push her back onto his bed.

"Luke, we can't," she said as she tumbled backward.

He covered her body with his. "Yes, we can."

His lips were on hers again, teasing, taunting, daring her to protest. How could she when her own traitorous hands had made their way under his shirt and were happily roaming over the taut, ripped muscles of his back?

He smelled so good. That scent that she thought of as purely Luke surrounded her, taking over her senses. It was a combination of clean soap and whatever amazing cologne he wore. She had to remember to ask him. Then his hand had undone the snap of her shorts and was inside her panties, and she couldn't remember anything.

Luke wasted no time inserting a finger inside her. She sighed loudly and deeply. He covered her mouth again with his, even as his finger was working its magic. She helpfully spread her legs for him, and he added a second finger. He knew just the right speed, just the right rhythm to drive her crazy.

She felt her body responding, could hear her breathing picking up, knew what was about to happen. Then Luke surprised her by backing off. He withdrew his hand and rose, standing over her at the bottom of the bed.

"Wh-what?" Her mind was hazy with the sudden loss of his touch.

"Don't worry, baby. I'm right here. Since we are in my mom's house, I thought this might not be the best opportunity to take our time." He reached into his back pocket, removing a condom.

He quickly shed his shorts and underwear, sheathed himself, and returned to her. Lola was still reeling and couldn't get herself to move from the bed. That didn't seem to be a problem for Luke. He simply removed her shorts and panties. Then he put his arms around her legs and gave one good tug, yanking her to the bottom of the bed.

"This is a much better angle." With that, Luke buried himself inside of her to the hilt.

The pressure was amazing. She loved the way he filled her so completely. She wanted to yell out, but Luke covered her mouth with his hand.

"Not this time, baby. We have to be quiet."

It was such a sexy feeling to be lying on his childhood bed, still completely clothed on the top but joined with him in such a primal way. His family was right downstairs as

Luke began to move in and out of her. He was standing at the bottom of the bed, still holding her legs, anchoring her right where he wanted her.

He had the perfect leverage to thrust into her, each time going even deeper until she could feel his balls banging against her. He was pumping his hips quickly now, intensifying their mating, upping the ante.

She couldn't scream, couldn't yell. She desperately wanted a release. She began to move her hips so she could meet him thrust for thrust. Using her muscles to tighten around his thick shaft, she stifled a laugh when he ground out an oath. Looks like he wanted to make noise as much as she did.

"Shh," she whispered with a twinkle in her eye as he continued to rock into her. "They'll hear us downstairs."

Her words seemed to ignite something inside of him. His hips moved at a greater speed; his fingers gripped her legs even tighter as he pushed into her. His grip would have hurt her if she wasn't experiencing such divine pleasure everywhere else.

Luke's eyes never left hers. Light streamed into the room, illuminating his face. He was so intense, so serious, as he brought her up the mountain of desire.

"Yes, that's it. Come for me, Lola."

"Yes, yes, Luke, just like that."

He was playing her just right, hitting all the right spots. He'd paid attention this last week, learning exactly what she liked. She hoped she could say the same about herself.

Her breasts felt heavy, and she was starting to sweat. A sensation began in her lower belly as Luke brought her exactly where she wanted to be. She came hard and fast, and Luke offered a triumphant smile. Then he thrust three more times and fell off his own cliff. As he did, she tightened around him as hard as she could.

"Oh fuck, Lola." He shuddered severely before collapsing on top of her.

"Wow," she cooed into his neck, taking a moment to lick the salty perspiration that had beaded there.

"Wow is right. How is it possible for it to get better every time?"

She had no clue. All she did know was that it was going to be difficult to put her clothes back on and walk downstairs like everything was normal, pretend Luke hadn't just rocked her world and devoured her body.

"Luke, Lola," Gwen yelled up the stairs. "What are you guys doing?"

"Nothing," they both answered at the same time. Their bodies were still joined, their voices still raspy.

"Food's on. Burgers have been placed on the grill. Although, I think you guys may have already started with dessert."

Lola groaned and Luke grinned. He placed a chaste kiss on her lips. "Welcome to the family."

Chapter Ten

"I'm depressed. I need a cookie."
-Sophia Petrillo

"Who's up for a little Marco Polo?"

Oliver's question was answered with a resounding round of no's and groans and then, since they were all hanging out in the pool, a chorus of splashing in his general direction.

"No one ever wants to have fun with me," Oliver said.

"I'll have some fun." Gwen jumped up. "Let's race."

Oliver grinned and rose up in the five feet of water. The sun glimmered off his tanned skin and muscled body. "You think you can take me?"

"I know I can," Gwen said.

"But you're a girl." Oliver stated this fact in a manner similar to a five-year-old. It had the desired effect though. Gwen gritted her teeth and stared him down.

"Let's go, fly boy. Prepare yourself to be embarrassed by a girl."

Mia clapped her hands together. "Yes. Lola can be the

judge. She's the only impartial one here."

"I don't know," Lola said. "I didn't care for the girl comment," she teased.

Luke emerged from the house, looking hot as hell in his blue swim trunks. He threw on a pair of shades and strutted toward the pool. Lola was pretty sure he'd hate that description, but she didn't care. She was having too good a time watching him.

"Earth to Judge Lola. Stopping ogling my brother."

Lola snapped to attention. Ugh. "I plead the fifth."

"We'll let it slide. This time," Mia warned with a smile. "Go sit over there on the steps. You are the eyes and ears of this race. Your final word is *the* word."

Lola half swam and half walked to the steps. "That's a lot of power. Hope it doesn't go to my head."

She made herself comfortable on the steps, enjoying feeling the hot sun on her skin, while she was halfway submerged in the cool water. Luke made his way to her.

"Hey, Lo, want to—"

She stopped him with a hand in the air. "Shh, I'm busy right now."

Laughing, he leaned down and placed a kiss on her shoulder. "So I don't need to be worried about you being alone with my family?"

"Stop distracting me. The race is about to start."

Luke perused the scene. "Ollie and Gwen are racing? My money's on Gwen." With that prediction, he rounded the pool and went to sit with his mom, who was under the large umbrella at one of the tables.

The race was fast and furious. Luke should have put money on it, because he'd been right. Gwen started off slow but when she made her move, Oliver didn't stand a chance. After that, Oliver needed to reclaim his man card by racing Mia, who did a doggy paddle across the pool.

Lola was still sitting on the steps of the pool, enjoying watching everything go down and partaking in her second— or was it third?—piña colada. Gwen swam over to her and perched herself next to Lola.

"Having fun?"

"So much. You guys are great. And it's fun to spend the day in a pool. We have one at my apartment building, but we always have to fight over getting a lawn chair and then there's always some kid screaming and then someone gets yelled at for having their music on too loud."

"Hashtag, first world problems," Gwen said with a wink.

"Totally." Lola laughed.

Gwen pushed her hair back and took a moment to glance around the backyard. Luke was still talking to his mom and aunt, Oliver and Mia were engaging in some kind of competition that Lola couldn't identify, and she had no idea where Winnie had run off to.

"I've been meaning to get you alone," Gwen said.

Uh-oh. Lola's mouth suddenly went dry.

Gwen didn't waste any time getting to it. "What's the deal?"

"The deal?" Lola repeated.

"With you and my brother."

"What do you mean? We're, you know, dating."

Gwen tilted her head, studying Lola. Then she swiveled to take in her brother across the patio. Finally, she shook her head. "Nope. I don't buy the whole meeting on a dating website."

"Lots of people meet online," Lola said, trying to divert the conversation.

"True and I have absolutely nothing against them. It's just...I can't see Luke going on one."

Good thing she was already in the pool because Lola would be sweating bullets about now. Instead, she wrung her fingers together. "How do you think we met?"

Gwen considered the question. "I'm not sure. But I do know it wasn't on Match or Tinder or whatever. The question is, why are you guys lying about it?"

Lola frantically tried to make eye contact with Luke. Clearly, he wasn't receiving her psychic message for help.

"So you don't think we're really dating?" Lola asked in a quiet voice.

"To be honest, no, I didn't think you were really dating. At least, not at first."

Lola shot her a questioning look.

Gwen shrugged. "You're not my brother's type. No offense, by the way. His type is usually heinous."

Finally, Lola chuckled. "Thanks for that."

"No prob. If I had to guess, I would say that Luke isn't your type either. Yet, I see the way the two of you look at each other." She gazed off in the distance for a long moment before blowing out a long breath of air. "There's something there, I know it."

"That's a good thing, right?"

"But there's a secret here, too. I can feel it."

Lola was torn. More conflicted than she'd been in a long time. On the one hand, she wanted to jump up and dance at the suggestion that she and Luke had something. But on the other, watching Gwen question her was horrible. She really liked Luke's sister.

She could feel the other woman's stare on her. Once again, she tried to silently beckon Luke to her side. And once again, it didn't work.

She was on her own.

"The truth is, Gwen..." Gwen leaned forward, her eyes intent on the next words out of Lola's mouth. "The truth is that I think it would be best for you to ask your brother any lingering questions. He's your family. I'm just some girl you met a week ago."

Clearly not the answer she wanted or expected, Gwen scrunched up her nose. "That's just it. This is only the second time my family has met you, and we all really like you."

"Thank you," Lola said around a throat thick with emotion.

"I like to make fun of Luke and give him hell. But the truth is that I really love my dumb brother. I don't want to see him get hurt. You're not going to hurt him, are you?"

Ever since she first met Gwen, Lola had been abundantly aware that she was the tough sister. Full of confidence and bravado and passion. But her question now was anything but. It showed her vulnerability.

"You know about my dad?" Gwen asked.

Surprised to be asked that question, Lola nodded.

"I think we're all still trying to get over that in our own way. Luke especially. Please don't hurt him."

Lola gulped down a large lump. "I wouldn't consciously hurt him. Please trust me on that. I wouldn't hurt any of you."

Only she'd just lied. She was going to hurt all of them when the truth came out. Her only hope was that Luke would change his stance on relationships.

Her mind wandered back up to his bedroom. Sure, they'd had sex. But it had been more than that, too. It had been special and magical.

The other morning she woke up cocooned in his arms. And he sent her texts throughout the day. Just checking up on her and saying hi. Little things that added up to one big gesture of caring.

They weren't being truthful to his family. But maybe there was a way out of it. Maybe they weren't pretending as much as they claimed. Maybe she could help Luke realize that a relationship with her wouldn't be the end of the world.

Maybe she was fooling herself. But damn if she wasn't

going to try.

. . .

Hell of a party.

Luke was having a great time. Maybe because it started off with some fun with Lola up in his bedroom. She was wearing the most appealing little pink bikini. He'd love nothing more than to snap his fingers, make everyone disappear, and then have his way with Lola in the pool. On the patio furniture. In the garden.

He caught her eye across the pool where she was talking to his sister. He offered a wink and she blushed.

Damn, he loved when she did that. He loved the way she looked. Loved the way she laughed. Loved…

Luke's grin faded, and he felt like he'd just been slammed against a brick wall. No way. He couldn't be in love with Lola or anyone else. He didn't allow himself to experience that emotion. No matter how great a girl's smile, laugh, body, heart was.

"What's with the frown?"

He snapped to attention at the sound of his mother's voice.

"What? Oh, nothing. Some stuff from work popped into my mind." He hated lying, but he didn't want to reveal to his mother that he wanted to make love to Lola all over her pristine backyard. Not to mention, he had no idea what to do with the feelings he was experiencing for her.

"More chips and guac?" his aunt asked.

"That would be great. Thanks." His mom watched his aunt make her way inside before turning to him. "I really like Lola."

"Ma, don't."

"Don't 'Ma, don't' me. I really like her."

"Stop."

"Nope," she said with a mischievous grin. The same expression he'd seen on his sisters millions of times.

"I don't want to talk about this."

"I'm your mother, and you will do what I say. Now, I think Lola is very sweet. Plus, she's just gorgeous."

No argument there. "She is."

"I can't believe she wasn't taken already."

He turned to watch her again. Lola and Gwen seemed to be in the middle of something serious. Their heads were close together, and they seemed to be speaking in hushed tones.

"She recently got out of a relationship," Luke said as he remembered Captain Douche Canoe who'd dumped her.

"That man's loss was our gain."

Luke felt his eyebrow rise at his mother's statement. "Our? How about my gain." Luke took a long drink of his piña colada.

"She's already part of the family."

The tropical drink stuck in his throat at his mother's words. Part of the family? Whose family?

"Uh, that's a bit much, Ma. Don't you think?"

"Not really. She gets along with everyone, and she's fun to be around." His mother reached across the table and patted his cheek, lingering for a moment. "She makes you happy. We can all see that."

They could?

Lorraine laughed. "You look like I just hit you in the face with my favorite cast iron skillet."

"I mean, this is a bit of a heavy talk for a pool party."

"Watching the two of you reminds me of myself and your father when we first met."

This time Luke's drink didn't get stuck in his throat because he was too busy spitting it out on the table. As he reached for a napkin to clean it up, he offered his mother his best what-in-the-fuck-are-you-talking-about look.

Lorraine simply laughed. "It wasn't always bad with your dad, Luke. We were very happy in the beginning. Very much in love."

"Oh yeah, I'm sure you were. Right up until he left you and his four kids and his house."

"Things changed. I used to focus all my energy on hating the situation and despising him. Guess what? That got me nowhere. Instead, I decided to remember the good parts." She pointed around the patio four times. "I got one son and three daughters from him. I learned that I could not only be a working mother but a damn good one. I took care of this house."

"But he didn't want to stay with us," Luke said.

"Again, that's not what I focus on. I remember how it was in the beginning. The romance and the wonder. Like what you have with Lola."

Luke wanted to throw his hands up in frustration. He didn't know how to process his mother's words, her revelation. His chest ached, and for a moment, the patio spun out of control. When it righted itself, there was Lola, standing up and drying off with a towel.

He liked her. A lot. Apparently his delinquent father had felt the same way about his mom. Then something changed. Something inexplicable.

How could someone go from feeling the way he was right now about Lola to the complete opposite? More importantly, what if he did the same thing to Lola?

What Luke realized in that moment was that he liked Lola way too much to ever hurt her.

• • •

Irked and irritated after his talk with his mom, Luke rose and stalked into the kitchen. He didn't really know why he'd come in here so he started opening and closing cabinets, searching for nothing. He moved down the counter until he was at the refrigerator. For good measure, he opened and closed that, too.

"Looking for something?"

Luke jumped. He hadn't heard Winnie come in. "I don't know," he answered honestly.

"Because in case you haven't noticed, we're having a party. There's enough food on the patio to feed a small country."

She jumped up to sit on the counter, a gesture she'd been doing since she was little. She also eyed him long and hard, another thing she'd been doing forever. Winnie was the sweetest of his sisters, but man, when she pinned him with that stare he felt like he was being interrogated in front of Congress.

"What?" he asked.

She tilted her head and one of her curls fell over her eye. She blew it out of the way. "You're acting weird."

"No, I'm not."

"Yeah, okay," she said, sarcasm coating her words.

He leaned against the opposite counter, crossed his legs at the ankles. "You're a pain in the ass."

"So you've been telling me since we were little, and yet you can't seem to get rid of me."

"But I'll keep trying."

Luke grinned. He loved all of his sisters but he particularly adored Winnie. There was a lovable innocence to her. She could ask him to jump off a building and he'd do it.

She jumped down off the counter. "I like Lola."

He felt his shoulders slump. "Me too."

"Do you like her? Or do you like-like her?" Winnie made a kissy face to go along with the question.

He threw an apple at her, which she easily caught.

"Well?" she asked.

"I like-like her," he said glumly.

"Then why are you frowning? Isn't that a good thing?"

"Win, do you ever think about Dad?" His question caught her off guard. Her eyes widened.

She shrugged. "I don't know. Not really. I mean, he's been out of our lives for so long now."

"Yeah, but he's still our dad."

"I guess. But I wasn't as close with him as you were. And Gwen. I know you two took it a lot harder than me and Mia. What made you bring him up? Especially when we were talking about your girlfriend."

If only she knew. Luke considered coming clean. He was well aware that Winnie would be the most understanding. In fact, he wanted to let loose. Tell her that Lola wasn't really his girlfriend. That they were just pretending. Only…

Only, Luke didn't think he was pretending anymore. He was feeling things for her. Real things. Heavy things. He like-liked her, as Winnie had put it. And he'd never been like this before with a woman. He'd liked his life like that. Simple. Uncomplicated. Free from the possibility of getting hurt. Free from hurting someone else.

If his dad had taught him one thing, it was that if you let yourself love another, they had the power to destroy you. They could walk away at any time. And then you were left with nothing, except memories and broken dreams.

"I feel like there's a lot happening in here." Winnie tapped a finger against his forehead. "Wanna talk about it?"

Yes! But he couldn't bring himself to utter that single word out loud.

He leaned forward and kissed her on the forehead. "Nah, not just yet. But thanks."

"You know how to reach me. If I'm not there, leave a

message with my assistant."

"You don't have an assistant."

"Shh." She grinned and started walking away. "I'm going to grab another one of Mom's fabulous piña coladas. See you outside?"

He nodded. "Win, watch out—" Too late, she turned the corner and ran smack dab into Oliver.

Luke watched as his sister and his best friend jumped backward as if they'd just run into a wall of fire.

"Sorry," they both uttered at the same time.

Then they did that dance where they both went to the right at the same time, then the left, then the right again. Finally, Oliver put his hands on Winnie's shoulders and moved her so he could pass on the left. Winnie's face turned a bright shade of red, and if he wasn't mistaken, so did Oliver's. Weird. What the hell was going on there? Winnie and Oliver had known each other most of their lives.

After Winnie let herself onto the patio, Oliver continued into the kitchen. He saw Luke and jumped. "Hey, man. Didn't know you were in here. I didn't do anything… I mean, I wasn't…Winnie just ran into me."

Was he drunk? Luke shook his head. "I know, I saw. Everything okay between you two?"

"There's nothing between us. I mean, uh, yeah. No. Why wouldn't everything be okay?"

"I don't know?" Luke finished that sentence as a question because for the life of him he had no idea what was happening.

Oliver grabbed two beers from the fridge. He handed one to Luke and then settled against the counter where Winnie had just been sitting. "Anyway, I should be asking you the questions. What's the deal, man?"

"The deal with what?"

"Come on." Oliver offered a "get serious" stare.

"You're going to have to be a little more specific."

"You and the sexy librarian."

Ah. Now he got it. "Lola?"

"Hell yes, Lola." He blew out a long whistle. "Man, she's something. Not your usual type though."

What was that supposed to mean? "What the hell, dude?"

"Get real. You typically go for the blonde space cadets with lots of highlights, too much makeup, and purchased boobs. Although, I have to say that behind the glasses and buttoned-up clothes, I happened to notice Lola has quite the impressive figure."

For the first time in his life, Luke understood the term blood boiling because he felt like his insides were on fire.

Oliver must have noticed something changed because he asked, "What? You've been spending all this time with her and you haven't noticed her body?"

"I'm not going to talk about her body."

"Why not?" Oliver honed in. Then he folded his arms over his chest and gave Luke a long once-over. "Wait a minute. Oh man."

"What?"

"This is serious."

"What?" Luke repeated, suddenly feeling like all the air had left his body.

Oliver threw his head back and laughed. "You've really fallen for the sexy librarian. Wow."

"No, no, no, it's not like that." Right?

"I never thought I'd see the day that commitment-phobe Luke Erickson would take a tumble into love."

Luke choked on the taste of beer he'd just thrown back. Coughing, he set the beer down on the counter. "You're full of it."

Oliver grinned. "Nope, you're full of it. Full of love. For Lola." He drew out her name, batted his eyelashes, and started making kissy noises.

"Shut the hell up. You don't know what you're talking about."

"Enlighten me then. I saw how you were looking at her. Plus, you did the protective hand on her back thing."

"The what? I think you've been watching too many Lifetime movies. Time to reclaim your man card."

"Fuck off," Oliver said good-naturedly. "But I know what I saw out there." He pointed toward the backyard.

"You know nothing. The whole thing between me and Lola is fake." Oliver lifted one eyebrow in obvious disbelief, so Luke kept going. "Seriously. I met Lola at our reunion. Remember? She and her crazy friend crashed it."

"What? Wouldn't have expected that out of her."

"She was coerced into it. But in any case, we started talking and we made a deal. I wouldn't out her at the reunion if she would pose as my girlfriend for my family reunion."

"Interesting." Oliver took a long pull of beer as he considered.

"You don't believe me?"

"I do. Speaking of Lifetime movies, this little plan is right up there. But answer me this. Your family reunion was last week. What is she doing here today?"

"She…well…" He sputtered a few more words before he finally fell quiet.

What the hell was he supposed to say? What did he even feel? Luke didn't want to think about it. He didn't want to acknowledge that Oliver made a good point. There was absolutely no reason to keep Lola around.

Except that he wanted her around.

He liked her being around.

He liked her. A lot. More than liked.

Maybe loved.

Oh shit.

"You know what I think?" Oliver asked. "I think that

during your little diabolical plan, you fell for her. I think you have some serious feelings for Ms. Lola McBride."

"Shut the fuck up. You have no idea what you're talking about." Having Oliver acknowledge the situation and his very real feelings for Lola made Luke want to lash out. "It's not real," he practically screamed.

"None of it?"

"None. I feel nothing for Lola." He shrugged, as if the words coming out of his mouth were true.

Only they weren't, and just saying them felt wrong. So very wrong. They left a bitter, acidic aftertaste on his tongue. Right then, he thought he heard something. It sounded like a strangled noise forced from the depths of someone. Probably just his mom's cat coughing up a fur ball. He listened closer but only heard the backdoor closing. He hadn't been aware anyone else was in the house.

An uneasy feeling settled in his stomach.

"Well, if that's the case, then maybe I'll ask her out."

Luke froze. "You'll ask who out?"

Oliver rolled his eyes. "How many beers did you have today? Who have we been talking about? Lola."

"You're going to ask Lola out?" Lola? His Lola? "Over my dead body," he said as his fingers curled into fists.

Once again, Oliver started to laugh. "Man, you have it bad." He grabbed his beer and slapped Luke on the arm. "I'll let you deal with that. See you back outside."

Luke took a moment, let his best friend's words sink in. He didn't know what to do. The only thing that seemed to make sense was to be with Lola. So he headed outside, anxious to talk to her. His steps were lighter as he entered the backyard.

After a quick perusal, he didn't see her so he sidled up to his mom.

"I saw you chatting with Oliver."

"Guys don't chat, Mom."

She laughed. "Excuse me. Did you two have fun?"

"It was…illuminating."

"What does that mean?"

"Never mind. Hey, have you see Lola?"

"No, honey. We were talking for a little bit. Then she went inside to the bathroom."

Inside? The hair on the back of his neck stood up straight.

Mia bounced over to them then. "Hey, what's wrong with Lola?"

Those hairs on his neck started to tingle. "What do you mean? I was just looking for her."

"She's out front. She looked really upset."

"Oh dear," Lorraine said.

"She said to apologize to you, Mom. She's leaving."

"Excuse me." Luke handed his beer to his sister and bolted for the door to the fence. He ran around the outside of the house and spotted Lola looking at her phone on the curb by the street.

"Lola, hey, Lola." He dashed up to her.

Lola glanced over her shoulder. Her eyebrows drew together, and she started walking in the opposite direction.

"Lola, wait."

"No," she called over her shoulder.

He thought he heard her say "not for you," but couldn't be sure with his heart hammering loudly in his ears.

Finally, Luke caught up to her. He grabbed her arm and spun her around to face him. "What are you doing out here? Where are you going?"

"I'm getting an Uber."

"Why?"

"So I can go home."

"Are you not feeling well?"

She pinned him with a hard stare. "I feel fine."

Her answers were all terse. He was getting nothing out of her. Even though he had no clue why she was leaving, Luke had a pretty good idea that she was pissed at him.

"Lola, please tell me what's wrong. You were having so much fun earlier."

"Was I?" she asked. "Hard to believe that since it's not real." She waved her arm at his mom's house, and then she moved her hand in between the two of them. "None of it."

His blood turned to ice as he recognized his own words being thrown back at him. He realized then that Lola had been in the house. She had overheard his conversation with Oliver.

"You heard me." His voice was soft and low. Suddenly, he felt like he was going to be sick.

"In the kitchen? With your best friend? Saying there was nothing between us? Um, yeah. I did hear that." She shook her head back and forth, her bangs swishing across her glasses. "I guess it's better to hear it now rather than later down the line when I'm even more invested in you and your family."

She clutched her phone even tighter. Luke could see her knuckles turn white.

"Lola…" But he didn't know how to finish that sentence. What could he say to make her understand?

She closed her eyes. "I'm such an idiot. Frankie tried to warn me."

"Warn you? About me?"

Her eyes flew open and she pushed him. Hard. "Yes, about you. How you would hurt me. And you did."

"I didn't mean—"

"You didn't mean to hurt me or you didn't mean what you said to Oliver in the kitchen?"

He saw hope spring into her eyes. She took a step forward.

"What I overheard in the kitchen, was it…just talk? Like

locker room kind of talk? Or did you mean it?"

This was it, an incredibly important moment. This could save his relationship with Lola.

He wanted to tell her he was afraid and that he'd just been mouthing off to his friend. He wanted to keep her here and not have her go away mad. But he also wanted to protect himself. His father's face flashed in his mind. All that pain washed over him.

"I meant what I said to Oliver."

Tears instantly formed in her eyes, but she took a few deep breaths and kept them from falling.

"Why did you sleep with me? If none of this is real, why have you spent every day with me for the last week?"

When she put it like that... She wasn't the idiot. He was. Only, he'd wanted to sleep with her because he was falling for her. He needed to tell her that, but he couldn't seem to get the words out.

"No reply." The disappointment on her face tore at something deep inside him.

"Look, Lola, I told you that I don't do this. I'm not made for relationships." Each word tasted bitter and wrong.

She checked her phone again. Then she shoved it in the pocket of her shorts. As she did, a car rounded the corner of the street. Her Uber.

Luke's pulse sped up. He only had a matter of seconds to talk to her before she got in that car and drove away. Drove out of his life. He had to make her understand, and he had to keep his heart from being broken again.

She began clapping. "Congratulations," she said bitterly, "you're just like your father, Luke."

He stepped back. "Excuse me?"

"You don't even see it, do you?"

"See what?"

"You think you're protecting yourself so you won't

get hurt again. But really, you're pushing everyone away. Everyone who wants to love you."

The car pulled up beside them. "One sec," Lola said to the driver.

"I am not like my father."

"Funny, from where I'm standing, you're pretty darn similar." Her eyebrows drew together in disgust. "He ran and so do you."

With that, she got in the car and slammed the door. Luke was too stunned to do much of anything besides allow his mouth to fall open in shock.

He wasn't the one running. Lola was the one in the car driving away from him. Just like his father had done all those years ago. His point had been proven. When you let someone in, they had the power to break your heart. Watching the car get smaller and smaller as it drove down the street, Luke felt sick. A part of him was in that car. With Lola.

With the woman he thought he loved.

Chapter Eleven

"No! No, I will not have a nice day!"
-Dorothy Zbornak

Luke had a headache the size of Virginia.

After Lola insulted him and hightailed it out of there, he'd stood at the curb, gawking after her Uber for a good five minutes. He couldn't believe what she'd said to him.

To make matters worse, he had to return to the backyard where everyone in his family was anxiously waiting to pounce on him.

Where's Lola?

Is everything okay, honey?

What happened?

Hope you didn't fuck that up.

That last comment had been from Gwen. Little angel that she was.

Now the hamburgers and hot dogs had been eaten, the dessert devoured, the sun had set, and it was dark outside. The barbeque had ended, and Luke was sitting around the fire pit with Gwen and Oliver. His friend hadn't asked any questions, but he'd stayed pretty close to Luke's side since Lola left. Oliver and Gwen were both uncharacteristically quiet, waiting for Luke to make the first move. Or the first sound.

But he wasn't ready to talk. Instead, he let his gaze drift over to the house. With the lights on inside, the whole place was illuminated. Luke could see his mom moving around the kitchen. Mia was helping her wash dishes and put food away.

He wasn't sure where Winnie had run off to. She had been sitting with him until Oliver joined them. Then she'd bolted faster than Lola.

Lola. His breath caught just thinking about her. Thinking about her words. He couldn't believe that she'd taken all of the things he'd shared with her about his father and threw them back in his face.

He swore under his breath.

That was exactly why he didn't open up to people. Once you did, they held all the power to hurt you, and Lola had succeeded beyond anything he could have imagined.

You're just like your father.

Luke grumbled.

He was nothing like the man who had walked out on his wife and four young children. The guy who stopped seeing his kids altogether. How could she even make that comparison?

Luke groaned.

"So are you gonna sit over there making weird guttural noises and the occasional oath, or are we going to talk about what happened tonight?" Gwen sat back against the cushion of the lawn chair she was occupying, as a smug smile spread across her face.

"Shut up."

"Oh, good comeback, dumbass. Don't get mad at me. I'm not Lola."

Oliver gave Gwen a very exaggerated once-over. "Nope, you're not. You're shaped all differently than her."

"Shut up," Luke repeated, only this time Gwen joined him. Oliver chuckled.

"She's right, though," Oliver said. "You might as well tell us what went down. We're going to find out anyway."

"And we're not leaving this fire of truth until you tell us," Gwen said.

He relented with a long sigh that was powerful enough to extinguish the fire of truth. "Lola overheard something that you and I were saying." He nodded at Oliver. "Next thing I know she ordered an Uber without so much as a goodbye, thanks for the party."

Gwen leaned forward. "That doesn't sound like her. I mean, I don't know her that well yet, but we had a pretty great talk today. And she doesn't strike me as the type of person to be rude like that."

"Guess you never really know someone," Luke said.

"I guess." But Gwen didn't seem satisfied.

"What made her leave?" Oliver asked.

Luke ran a hand over his face. "It's not what made her leave. It's what she said when she did leave. She told me that I was just like my dad." Not wanting to meet his sister's eyes, he dropped his gaze to the ground.

"Excuse me? She said what?" He would have been able to hear the shock and irritation in Gwen's voice a mile away. "How dare she talk about a private family issue that she knows absolutely nothing about. Especially after I talked to her about it."

"Exactly." Luke felt vindicated. Although, he really needed to clarify it a bit. "Well, actually, she does know some of it." Gwen's mouth dropped. "She knows the whole story. Because I kind of told her about it."

"You told her about your dad?" Oliver cracked his

knuckles. "You never talk about that," he said.

"Yeah, well, we were getting to know each other. It was kind of nice to share it. Plus, she wanted to know why I don't do relationships. I had to explain it. She was really understanding." Until she threw it back in his face. "Then she goes and uses it against me."

"But why?" Gwen demanded. "Why did she even say that?"

Luke shook his head. "Oliver was giving me shit in the kitchen about Lola. I told him it wasn't real between us."

"Not real, sure," Oliver interrupted. "You're sitting out here with us moaning away after the girl, and it's totally fake."

"Can I finish?" Luke groaned again. "Lola heard what I said, and she left. When I talked to her out front, she said that I was just like Dad, always leaving, always running away."

Now Gwen was shaking her head. "Wow."

"Exactly. I told you she was out of line."

"Not wow to Lola. Wow to you. You are a huge jerk."

"Excuse me?"

"Dad really did a number on you. I mean, I thought I was bad." Gwen whistled. "But you are ten times worse than I am."

"She hurt me," he ground out between his clenched teeth.

"You can't get hurt by someone if they don't mean anything to you," Oliver said. "Just sayin'."

Gwen ignored him. "I'm pretty sure you hurt her, too. Can you imagine what she felt when she overheard you and your idiot-compadre here? No offense," she said to Oliver.

"None taken."

"I mean I really, really, and I can't emphasize this enough, *really,* don't want to hear about your sex life or even think that you have sex. However, I have to assume that you and Lola, you know, did it."

She waited, pinning him with a questioning stare.

Through the flames of the fire, Gwen's sharp features looked even more intense, and Luke wanted to hide. He only hoped that his sister wouldn't be able to tell that his face was burning up with what had to be a deep blush. He nodded silently in answer instead.

"Let me get this right then. I'm going to lay out all the details. You meet Lola."

"She looked so hot that night," Oliver added.

Gwen pointed a stern finger in his direction. "Don't make me come over there." She coughed. "As I was saying, you two come up with this insanely stupid plan to pretend to be together so we'll all get off your case."

"It *was* stupid, I kn—"

Gwen stopped him with a hand. "I get why you did it. I know we have a tendency to be a bit, ahem, annoying."

"A bit," Luke said.

"Somewhere along the lines of getting to know each other for this ruse, you actually fall for her and she falls for you. Then you sleep with her, invite her to more family functions, and then lie—again—by telling your moronic best friend that you don't have any feelings for her. And she overhears you saying this."

When she put it like that…

Luke was a gigantic piece of crap. Lola should have had the Uber run over him.

What he didn't dare tell either of them was that he'd also gotten to know Lola. It wasn't just that Lola wanted a family of her own in the future. It was that she didn't currently have one at all. He told her he was there for her, that she could count on him.

What does he go and do? Yanks that promise away from her at the first opportunity.

"We all know you like her, Luke." Gwen moved over to join him on his lawn chair.

"He more than likes her. He loooovvves her," Oliver said.

Gwen sighed. "I honestly don't know why I hang out with you." She turned to Luke. "That's not a bad thing, either. It's okay to have a girlfriend. It's okay to get married someday. It's okay to be in a relationship."

"But Dad—"

"Was a selfish prick," Gwen finished. She shrugged. "Doesn't mean you have to be."

"What are you talking about?"

"I get what Lola said to you. I understand it. And she was right too. Dad hurt you so badly. You in turn shut yourself off from almost everyone in your life so you won't get hurt again. Even though you're not physically running from her, you're emotionally leaving her in the dust. That makes you Dad junior."

"Hey, that's spot on," Oliver said.

"Furthermore..." Gwen was on a roll now. "It's like you're trying to stick it to Dad by not letting Lola in. But, really, you're punishing yourself."

Luke felt like his sister had taken the grill and slammed it against his face. He wasn't punishing himself by... He sat back and closed his eyes. And all he could see was Lola's sad, disappointed face staring back at him.

Shit.

He was punishing himself. And Lola. All because he didn't want to be like his dad.

"Here's the real question, bro. Do you want to be with her?"

His attention snapped up at Gwen's question. "Huh?"

She leaned toward him and emphasized each word. Slowly. "Do-you-want-to-be-with-her?"

"It's not a hard question," Oliver said.

No, it wasn't. In fact, it was the easiest question he'd ever been asked.

Did he want to be with Lola? A gorgeous woman who was smart and funny and sweet and kind. He enjoyed talking to her. Then there was their physical connection, which continued to blow his mind. He felt a grin spreading across his face as he remembered their earlier activity in his bedroom.

"You know, Oliver, I think that's a yes," Gwen said.

"I believe it is." Oliver chuckled.

"Hey, when did you get so smart?" Luke asked his sister with a playful shoulder nudge.

"Eh, I have my moments."

"Can you do me a favor?"

She started laughing.

"Do you know what I'm going to ask?" Luke said with amusement in his voice.

"Of course. You just said how smart I am." She pretended to huff on her fist and then wipe it against her shirt. "I won't tell Mia or Winnie about the whole pretend girlfriend thing."

"And I won't tell them that I love you the most."

"You're such a faker." She shoved him. "So how are you going to fix this?"

Luke whipped out his cell and shook it in front of Gwen. "This little bad boy is going to help me."

He scrolled through his contacts until he found the name he wanted. Then he connected and waited anxiously for the other person to pick up. He thought it was about to go to voicemail when a very feminine voice answered.

"I can't believe you're calling me."

"Hey, Frankie. I need your help."

· · ·

Lola didn't know why she'd let herself be dragged out of the house and all the way into D.C. to go to a stupid club when all she really wanted to do was stay in bed and hide under the covers until she was fifty-seven years old.

This had been the worst week ever. Work had dragged on and on. She'd totally messed up a project she'd been working on for her boss. Her team had lost at their weekly bocce game. Not to mention all of the questions and comments she'd received regarding Luke. A subject she really, really didn't want to talk about.

Not that Frankie had cared. Her bestie had hounded her all week long.

"Come on, Lo. Just talk to me."

"I'll talk to you as long as we don't talk about Luke."

"But…"

"But nothing. I don't want to talk about him."

"But how are you feeling?"

"Like crap. Lies are always bad. I should have known better. He used me. The asshole was using me all along."

"But how do you know?"

"I told you. I overheard him telling Oliver that nothing between us was real." She put her head down. *"I should have listened to you. You were so right."*

Frankie sighed. *"No, I wasn't, Lo."*

"You said I would get hurt and guess what? I'm hurt."

"What if he didn't mean it?"

"Ugh. Frankieeeeee, I don't want to keep discussing this."

"Lola, you have to."

To get Frankie off her back, she finally spit out her feelings. *"I miss him. Okay? I really miss Luke. Are you happy now?"*

Frankie had glanced at her cell phone for a long moment. Then she'd smiled and mumbled something along the lines of, "That's all I needed to hear."

Whatever. Lola was exhausted. She didn't want to spend her coveted Friday night at the newest club in D.C. wearing one of Frankie's shirts that was way too tight and cutting off her circulation. That said nothing about her feet, which were killing her, and it was only one hour into this dreaded outing.

Why did Frankie think that when she was upset, the cure-all was going out? The real solution would have been for her to dress up in her favorite pair of comfy pajamas, snuggle into her bed, and watch mindless reality television until she finished a pint of her favorite ice cream and drifted off into a dreamless sleep.

But no. Instead, she was busy trying to flee the dance floor, even as this guy who could clearly not get a hint—or her straight-up telling him that she didn't want to dance—continued to try and grind on her. Even as he was chasing her.

If she hadn't been so depressed, she probably would have laughed at the walking-grinding motion he was doing. He resembled a broken horse with hiccups.

Finally, she made it to the ladies' room, where broken horse man couldn't get to her. She brushed her hair, even though she really couldn't care less about her appearance. Then she waited for fifteen minutes, hoping her dancing friend had moved on.

She peeked her head out the door and saw that the coast was clear. She made her way to the bar. Frankie came bouncing over.

"Isn't this place great? Do you want another pomegranate martini?"

Lola pinned her with a stare. "No. I'm going home."

"Oh, Lola."

She stuck a hand out. "Don't try to stop me. I don't want to be here. I shouldn't have come out at all."

Frankie's eyes softened. "I'm not going to stop you, but I am going to come with you."

"Frankie, you don't have to do that. You're not the one in mourning."

"Neither are you. He's just a guy."

Her stomach cramped. Luke wasn't just a guy; he was *her*

guy. Or, he was, for a short time, but still. She missed that. Missed him. How was it that she hadn't even known him that long and yet she couldn't stop thinking about him?

"I'm going to tell Hannah and Celeste that we're leaving. Hang tight."

Twenty minutes later, they were out on Pennsylvania Avenue. Lola's ears were ringing, and her toes were aching. She could not wait to get back to their apartment.

"Thanks for leaving with me."

"Of course."

"I know you wanted to stay." Lola did feel bad.

"You can make it up to me."

Lola tilted her head. "How?"

"Take a walk with me."

Was she kidding? She'd be lucky if she made it to the curb in these devil shoes.

As if reading her mind, Frankie reached into her purse and produced a pair of flip-flops. "Here, put these on."

"Why do you have those in your bag?"

"Always be prepared."

Lola laughed. "Fine. Since it's actually cooler than a hundred degrees and the humidity isn't making me feel like killing myself, I guess I can go for a walk with you. But you're a weirdo."

"Love you, too." Frankie beamed. "Let's stroll down to the monuments."

"The monuments? Are you kidding? It's summer. It'll be packed with tourists." More dreaded than mosquitos, tourists flocked to the nation's capital every summer, forcing the natives to stay in their respective neighborhoods.

"Nah, it's too late for them. They're already tucked into their beds in their overpriced hotels. Come on." She pulled Lola's arm and started hightailing it down the street.

Finally, they made it across Constitution Avenue and

began walking toward the Reflecting Pool. Lola had to admit that she did love being down here. There was something almost peaceful about it. Even as cars whizzed by on either side of them, cutting each other off, and honking their horns. Even with the usual hustle and bustle of the city.

"Let's walk all the way to the Lincoln," Frankie said excitedly.

"You'd think you'd never seen it before," she said, amused at her friend who was practically bouncing with enthusiasm.

"I feel like tonight's special."

Lola stopped herself from rolling her eyes. "It started off with a crazy, smarmy man trying to grind up on me during a remix of a Katy Perry song. I don't know how it can get better than that."

"Surprises happen every day."

They continued walking along the Reflecting Pool in silence. Lola was happy to see that Frankie had been right. Most of the tourists were gone for the day.

They climbed the white marble steps of the Lincoln Memorial. Right before they reached the top, Lola turned around and took in the scene.

The D.C. monuments at night.

She sighed. This was how her parents had spent their first night together. Taking in the glittering lights and majestic beauty that distinguished Washington, D.C. from anywhere else in the world.

How lucky her parents had been. Both of their lives had been cut short. But at least they'd found each other. All of those years together with the one you loved.

Sadness fell over her like the warm breeze that was falling over the tree-lined streets.

Luke said that he would be there for her. That she wasn't alone. But in the end, she was alone. Utterly and completely alone.

No boyfriend.

No Luke.

No family.

That was the hardest part. Lola felt like she'd gotten a taste of something wonderful. Something she could really be a part of. Then it was stripped away from her.

Not for the first time, she chastised herself. How could she be so stupid? So naive. So gullible.

In the end, she couldn't blame him fully. Not the way she wanted to. Because Lola got it. He'd shared his relationship and falling out with his father. She couldn't even imagine having a parent who didn't care, who left you at such a young age.

Of course, Luke would have issues. She only wished that he'd let her help him with those issues instead of pushing her out. She'd been fully aware that what she'd said to him out on the curb in front of his mother's house had been cruel. He needed to hear it, though. Maybe it would help. Maybe not.

"Hey, what is that?"

Lola looked behind her where Frankie was pointing. She didn't see anything. "Where?"

"Up there. On the top landing."

Lola walked up the last couple of steps. "I don't see any…"

Luke.

Her heart stopped beating for a full second. Then it started up again, thumping wildly, moving double-time.

She stood there. As motionless as the large statue of Abraham Lincoln towering over Luke.

"Hi," he said. He shoved his hands in his pockets, offered her a bashful grin.

"Hey," she said so softly, she wasn't sure he'd heard her. But then he took a step forward. "What are you doing here?"

Frankie coughed delicately behind her. Lola swung

around and took in her best friend's very guilty face.

"You did this? You set this up?"

"Guilty," Frankie said with a shrug.

Lola's head was spinning. "But the club and going out tonight…"

Frankie grinned. "All a ruse to get you out of the house."

She looked between her best friend and Luke. "You two have been talking?"

"It took me days to wear her down," Luke offered.

Lola spun around again until her gaze connected with Frankie's. Her best friend had moved down to the next landing, wearing a big grin on her face. She nodded and gave a thumbs-up. Then she retreated into the night, leaving her alone with Luke.

Nerves threatened to overtake her. After what happened between them the week before at his mother's house, she'd assumed she'd never see him again.

"Hey," she repeated.

"Lola, I…that is, I mean, uh." He shook his head. "I'm not doing a very good job here."

"You wanted to see me tonight?"

"Yes. Actually, I wanted to see you every day for the last week."

"Why?"

His harsh words came back to her.

It's not real.

I feel nothing for Lola.

She swallowed. Hard. Why on earth would he want to see her if those words were true. Unless…

"I'm so sorry, Lola."

She didn't want to get her hopes up. This could all be too good to be true.

She took him in, from head to toe. Dark circles were under his eyes, and he needed to shave. He looked a mess. In fact, he seemed the least polished she'd seen him since they met.

Was it possible he'd been feeling as crappy as she had all week? But those words...

Lola bit her lip and considered. Maybe she would make him work for this a bit more.

"What are you sorry for?"

"Everything." The word shot out from his mouth. "Christ, Lola, I can't believe you overheard what I said to Oliver."

She frowned and angled away from him. They were at the top of the Lincoln Memorial. The view was spectacular from here. The whole National Mall was laid out before them. How many people came here, to this city, to this spot, with dreams and hopes and wishes?

Well, she had dreams of her own. A husband, children, a family.

Luke came into her life and gave her a brief glimpse into the future that she would give anything to get. Then he ripped it away before she could tell him how she was feeling.

She faced him again. "I can't believe you said that to Oliver."

"Lola," he began, but stopped.

"You never really know what's going on in another person's mind, I guess. But I was getting the impression that things were a certain way between us. Or, at least, headed in a certain direction."

He closed the distance between them, took her hands in his. Having him this close, being able to soak in that special Luke smell, defeated her senses. She let him hold onto her.

"We were headed in that direction." He squeezed her fingers tightly to emphasize his words.

"But what you said was so mean, so hurtful."

"And so very untrue."

She gasped. "What? Then why did you say it?"

"Because I'm a dick. Because my best friend, who I've known for a million years, knows exactly how to get under my skin. Oliver could see how I was falling for you. So he was goading me." He took a moment. "I have issues, Lola. Deep-rooted issues tied to my dad. I recognize that now. I took out my issues on you."

Her heart hurt for him. "I understand why you're scared, Luke. I really do." She took a deep breath. "I know I said something really hurtful to you, too. I'm sorry."

"You were right."

His words shocked her.

"What?" she said on a strangled laugh.

"You were right. I was acting like my dad. I found myself getting close to you, and it scared me, so I ran. But I'm not running anymore."

No, he wasn't. He was standing with her, holding her hands tightly, and begging her to… What?

"What are you saying, Luke?"

"That I'm sorry and that I want to be with you. In such a short time, you've come to mean so much to me, Lola."

"Oh, Luke, you mean so much to me, too."

Then he kissed her. Feeling his mouth against hers again erased all of the angst and turmoil she'd been dealing with that week. She twined her arms around his shoulders, and his wrapped around her back, pulling her even closer.

Their mouths fused together for what seemed like hours. But she couldn't get enough of his taste, his smell, his touch. When the kiss ended, they stayed entwined and both broke out into huge grins.

"I can't believe we just did that here," Lola said.

"Hey, if I want to kiss my girlfriend in public, then that's what I'm going to do."

"Your super-secret, pretend girlfriend?" She winked.

He shook his head. "Nope, not anymore. My very real,

super-amazing girlfriend."

Her heart felt like it was full to bursting. It couldn't be fair for one person to feel this happy.

She tilted her head and nodded in the direction of the Reflecting Pool. The Washington Monument stood tall in the background, surrounded by flags. The dome of the Capitol sat beyond that. "It's beautiful, isn't it?"

"What was it that your parents said? Everyone should see the monuments at night…"

"With someone you love," she finished. As soon as the words left her mouth, she slapped a hand to it.

Luke nodded and pulled her to him. "Yes, Lola. I love you."

"You do?" She felt the tears stinging the back of her eyes.

"Oh yeah."

Now she let the tears fall. "That's really great, because I love you, too."

They stayed right where they were the entire night. They watched the glittering display of the historic monuments as they talked for hours on end. The full moon shone in the Reflecting Pool, offering a light.

And they talked and talked, not stopping until they realized it was morning. Then they watched the sunrise over the nation's capital.

"I like seeing the sunrise with you."

"Then get used to it. There's going to be a lot more of them."

He grabbed her hand, entwining their fingers, and brought it to his lips for a kiss. Then they rose and walked down the white marble steps, headed toward their new future together, which was just as shiny as the monuments at night.

Epilogue

"Another reunion."

Lola smiled. She could practically hear the *ughhhhhh* emanating from Luke's words.

She squeezed the hand she was holding and stopped outside of her apartment door. "It's not that bad."

"It's my family."

"I happen to like the whole Erickson clan, and I'm looking forward to another shindig tomorrow."

He pulled her in for a quick kiss. "Are you sure you're not sick of us yet?"

Tilting her head from left to right, Lola pretended to consider the question. "Your family's great. You, on the other hand…"

"Hey, didn't I just take you out to a nice anniversary dinner? I'm a great guy." He leaned toward her and whispered, "And still the hottest guy you've ever seen."

That was for damn sure. Lola could barely believe they'd known each other for an entire year. Three hundred and sixty-five days of being with a gorgeous, intelligent, funny, sweet, incredibly sexy, no-longer-fake, but totally real, boyfriend.

It was too good to be true.

And a boyfriend who had insisted on taking her for a one-year anniversary dinner tonight. How romantic was that?

"Your looks are okay, but I'm really using you for your body."

Luke faked a shocked expression. "I knew it."

She laughed. "Seriously, though, dinner was great. Now," she continued winding her arms around his neck, "why don't we go inside for a little dessert? Frankie said she would be out late tonight."

"Well, actually—"

She cut him off by pressing her mouth to his. What she'd meant to keep light and fun quickly turned passionate. Like it always did with them.

Minutes later, they broke apart, panting. She wiped a finger over his lips, removing her lipstick. She noticed he sent a text and wondered who in the world he could be texting at this particular moment.

Luke took her key from her and unlocked the door. Then he stepped back and gestured for her to go in first.

Lola pushed open the door and crossed the threshold. She reached for the lamp that they kept on a table next to the door and turned it on.

"Surprise!"

Surprise was right. She fumbled backward as people jumped out from every available space in the small apartment.

"What the...?"

Her eyes darted from one side to the next, taking in all of the people. Frankie was there, and it looked like most of the bocce girls. Luke's mom was beaming as she stood in the doorway to the kitchen. Mia, Winnie, and Gwen were all throwing confetti. A large sign strung above the couch read *Happy Anniversary!*

"Luke!" she exclaimed. "Did you do all of this for me?"

He shoved a hand through his hair, hair that was slightly longer than when she'd met him last year. "Well, I had some help."

"No need to thank me, Lo." Frankie bounced across the room and threw her arms around Lola. "Happy one year anniversary, bestie."

"I don't know what to say." Good thing so many people were hugging and congratulating her. She didn't really have time to speak.

When the excitement started to die down, Lola noticed a table set up with an array of different colored cupcakes. Surely, Mia had baked them. She couldn't wait to taste one.

There were also drinks and cookies and chips. All the essential food groups.

Crossing to Luke, who was talking to Oliver, she grabbed him and kissed him firmly. "Thank you so much for all of this, but I thought we were being low-key for our anniversary."

He hugged her tightly. "You deserve so much more than low-key. Besides, do you think my mom and sisters would really let this momentous occasion go by without a celebration?"

She grinned. Over the last year, she'd become so close with Luke's mom and sisters.

"Like it or not, you're family now," Winnie said.

Lola's heart felt like it could burst from her chest any minute. Joyful tears threatened, but she was able to hold them at bay.

She had a family again.

"There's something else," Luke said and nodded at Frankie, who smiled and then vanished from the living room.

"What else could there be? This is more than I could have hoped for."

"Don't speak so soon."

Lola turned at her roommate's voice. She was about to ask what Frankie meant, but the words froze in her throat as she noticed that Frankie was carrying something small and fuzzy in her arms. When the ball of fur started wriggling, Lola realized that Frankie held a dog.

Not just a dog. A puppy.

"Oh. My. God. A puppy," she squealed.

She ran to Frankie, arms wide open. Frankie put the tan puppy in her arms. The dog settled down immediately. His little pink tongue darted out of his mouth and licked her. "Ohhh, he's so sweet." He had a light brown nose and what appeared to be greenish eyes. He definitely had some poodle in him, but she wondered what else.

"Whose dog is this?" she asked the room at large.

Luke stepped up behind her. "Yours, if you'll have her. It's a girl."

"Mine?" She looked down at the puppy's adorable face and fell in love instantly. "I can't believe...oh. I can't believe you did this," she said with a sad voice. "We can't have a dog here."

Her heart fell. She snuggled the puppy to her chest.

The room seemed to grow extra quiet. There was definitely something in the air. Lola glanced around, wondering what she was missing. "What's going on?"

Luke nodded at Frankie again.

"Do you like her collar?" Frankie asked.

What a weird question to ask at this moment. "Yeah, it's great." Lola quickly glanced down at the pink and white polka dot collar. Then she did a double-take. "What is this?" She wrapped her fingers around a gold key that was latched onto the collar.

"It's the key to my place," Luke announced. "To, um, our place."

"Our place?"

"If you'll have me, because I would really love for you and our new puppy to move in with me."

Lola could barely believe what she was hearing. She locked eyes with Frankie who grinned and mouthed *It's okay*. Then she saw that Luke's family was all smiles. Her friends were watching her with excitement on their faces.

The puppy let out a little *arf*. That was all she needed to hear.

"Yes," she said.

Luke let out a *whoop* and picked her and the puppy up and twirled them around. The room exploded into applause.

Later, much later, when the party began to die down, Lola found herself alone in a corner with her new roommate. Luke rubbed a hand over the puppy's back, ruffling her fur. Lola placed a kiss on her head.

"Happy?"

More than she'd been in a long, long time. She had an amazing boyfriend, a family, a brand-new puppy, and a life that she couldn't wait to start living.

"Very." She kissed him. "You really turned out to be the best pretend boyfriend."

He kissed her back. "Good. I hope to be the last."

. . .

Kennedy High School
15-Year Reunion Roundup

What have the Bobcat alums been up to over the last five years?

Luke Erickson

Current Residence: Arlington, VA
Career: Architect
Spouse: Lola McBride Erickson
Pastimes: Rogue bocce league and hanging with family
Kids: Twin daughters, Rose & Sophia
Pets: Two dogs, Blanche & Dorothy
Quote: *"The older you get, the better you get. Unless you're a banana."* –Rose Nylund

Acknowledgments

I'd like to thank the entire team at Entangled Publishing for all their hard work and long hours, especially my editor Alethea Spiridon who has been so amazingly supportive. Of course, I send glittery kisses to my agent. Nic, I love you!

A big shout-out to my real-life rogue bocce team: Julie, Trina, Ashling, Ginnie, Victoria, Mikaela, Nikki, Kristin, and Max, Maura and Eleanor, too. Go Team A or B or 1 or 2 or Ikea or Christmas! Thanks for welcoming me into the group and for adding some fun to my summers!

A huge thank you to my family and friends. To my fur-baby Harry, I can't imagine writing a book without you sleeping under my desk, or, on occasion, lounging across my laptop.

To Jen-Jen and Katinka and the infamous sangria-filled BBQ singing *The Golden Girls* theme song. Sorry, neighbors!

Lastly, I'd like to thank my Nunnie, who not only decided I would be a writer when I was a little girl, but also introduced me to many things I probably shouldn't have been watching at an early age. Thank you for the introduction to Dorothy, Rose, Blanche, and Sophia. You were right, they were ahead of their time. And I treasure those Saturday night sleepovers laughing at the TV. I miss you!

About the Author

Award-winning romance author Kerri Carpenter writes contemporary romances that are sweet, sexy, and sparkly. When she's not writing, Kerri enjoys reading, cooking, watching movies, taking Zumba classes, rooting for Pittsburgh sports teams, and anything sparkly. Kerri lives in Northern Virginia with her adorable (and mischievous) rescued poodle mix, Harry. Visit Kerri at her website, on Facebook, Twitter, or Instagram, or subscribe to her newsletter.

Find love in unexpected places with these satisfying Lovestruck reads...

THREE DAY FIANCEE
an *Animal Attraction* novel by Marissa Clarke

Between helicopter pilot Taylor Blankenship's job, his dog, and his matchmaking grandmother, he has no time for anyone or anything—especially a woman. The job of New York City dog walker suits Caitlin Ramos perfectly while she preps for her CPA exam. Men suck. Especially her bossy, hot client with the Saint Bernard that thinks it's a lap dog. Offered a bargain she can't refuse, Caitlin finds herself playing the part of fiancée to Taylor. All she has to do is fake a relationship with Mr. Bossy Pants in front of his entire family and not lose her heart to a guy who turns out to be a lot more than she'd bargained for.

JUST ONE SPARK
a novel by Jenna Bayley-Burke

Firefighter Mason has searched his whole life for a woman who stirs his soul. When he finds her, she's nose-deep in a racy paperback atop a vibrating washer. He's rushed into fiery situations before, and this woman is totally worth the risk. He'll just have to prove to Hannah that first impressions can be wrong and their spark of attraction is oh so right.

THE BEST FRIEND INCIDENT
a *Driven to Love* novel by Melia Alexander

Stacey Winters's best friend Grant offers her a window into the male psyche—and sets the bar high for her future Mr. Right. But then she accidentally crosses the friend zone and kisses him. Grant Phillips doesn't do relationships. "No attachments" is his hard and fast rule. There's only one exception: his best friend, Stacey. But now that he knows how good it felt to kiss her, felt the addictive slide of her body against his, Stacey Winters is indelibly stamped onto Grant's brain—and not just as his friend.

ONE LITTLE KISS
a *Smart Cupid* novel by Maggie Kelley

Love blogger Kate Bell is finished with men—*especially* the hot ones. Of course her only chance to save her career requires snagging an interview with the man who literally wrote the book on love, reclusive and super-sexy relationship expert Jake Wright. Who happens to be her boss's brother.

Made in the USA
Middletown, DE
03 April 2025

73727127R00118